"PATH OF HOLINESS" COLLECTION

Echoes of Wounds

AND THE ENCOUNTER THAT HEALS

VICTOR M. ROMERO C.

This book, titled **"ECHOES OF WOUNDS – And the Encounter That Heals,"** is based on the original Spanish work **"LOS ECOS DE LAS HERIDAS – Y El Encuentro Que Sana,"** registered with the U.S. Copyright Office under case number 1-15155629981.

Date of submission: May 4, 2026.
Pending registration with the U.S. Copyright Office.
Type of work: Literary.

This book is part of the "**PATH OF HOLINESS**" **COLLECTION**, dedicated to spiritual formation, soul restoration, and prophetic discernment in the end times.

Any resemblance to real persons, places, or events has been approached with respect and spiritual intention.
This work has been consecrated as an instrument of light, teaching, and pastoral calling.

ISBN (Spanish Edition): 979-8-9937568-8-2
ISBN (English Edition): 979-8-9937568-9-9

Cover design and editing: Victor Manuel Romero Celis
Printed in the United States of America

"This work is a fiction novel inspired by ancient stories in the public domain.
The characters, dialogues, and extended scenes are the original creation of the author."

For contact, collaborations, or access to additional content, scan the QR code on the back cover.

A Hidden Wound Can Never Be Healed...

Exposure of the Wound Is Necessary for complete Healing...

Even if it hurts at first, its benefits will be enjoyed in the end...

DON'T HIDE YOUR WOUNDS ANY LONGER!!

... RECEIVE THE HEALING OF YOUR SOUL

GENERAL CONTENTS

INTRODUCTION

"ECHOES OF WOUNDS - AND THE ENCOUNTER THAT HEALS"

This work is a novel—a story woven between the real and the imagined, between what happened and what could have happened, between the silences of an ancient woman and the voices of so many women today.

It does not seek to reconstruct an exact past, but to reveal a human heart that could belong to any of us.

Although the characters and scenes move within the realm of fiction, the wounds that run through these pages are profoundly real: abandonment, shame, invisibility, emotional abuse, heavy silences, and burdens carried for years.

And the possibility of an encounter that changes everything is also real—as real as the air we breathe.

This book was born from the desire to show how the Voice of God, when it breaks into the midst of the personal desert, can heal what once seemed impossible to heal.

How a single encounter can straighten a twisted destiny, restore a lost dignity, and return to a woman—any woman—the name that life once took from her.

Here you will find words that seek to touch ancient wounds, voices that accompany, scenes that embrace, and a Messenger who continues to speak in places where no one else dares to enter.

This story is not only Hagar's, nor only Eliana's. It is the story of every woman who has ever walked with a broken soul and discovered that God had not forgotten her.

If you have ever carried pain for too long, if you have ever run without knowing where to go, if you have ever felt your name fade away…

…this book is for you.

Because there are still wells in the desert...

Still The Messenger calls by name...

And there are still encounters that restore dignity.

Victor Manuel Romero Celis

Chapter 1

"THE BOOK"

The Words That Invited Her on a Journey

New York had always had a noise of its own— a noise that sometimes didn't come from the city, but from the wounds a person carries without knowing it.

A noise that doesn't ask permission. A noise that imposes itself. A noise that settles into the bones.

That afternoon, the bustle was louder than usual. Taxis honked as if competing with each other. Sirens crossed the avenue like red and blue arrows. Street vendors shouted offers no one heard. Tourists hurried without knowing where they were going.

But the loudest noise wasn't outside…It was inside.

Eliana walked to work with the feeling that each step reminded her of something she didn't want to think about.

The city's noise mirrored the noise in her soul—chaotic, confused, uncomfortable, relentless. A noise that wasn't silenced by sleep, work, or quiet. A noise begging to be heard.

Eliana entered the restaurant. The noise changed, but it didn't lessen.

Plates clattering. Cutlery falling. Orders shouted from the kitchen. Overlapping conversations. Laughter that wasn't hers. Music no one truly listened to.

She tied her apron. Pulled her hair back. Took a deep breath and continued.

She waited tables as if repeating a learned ritual. Smiling without feeling. Listening without hearing. Walking without being present.

A woman present in body, but absent in soul.

Meanwhile, a wind swept through the buildings of New York— a free, wandering wind. Its friction against the structures produced a hum that announced its presence, moving as if searching for someone among the many… as if carrying an ancient message, an echo that had crossed centuries to find her.

Until he arrived.

An elegant man— not elegant because of his clothes, but because of the way he occupied space. Calm. Confident. Quiet. As if the noise of New York couldn't touch him.

He sat at a table by the window. Ordered coffee. Nothing more.

Eliana served him without looking too closely. She had learned not to look at men. Not to give them space. Not to open doors.

But he looked at her. Not with desire. Not with judgment. Not with pity. With recognition.

A gaze that didn't ask, didn't invade, didn't demand.

It simply saw.

As if he had been searching for her and waiting for her at the same time.

When he finished his coffee, Eliana approached to take the cup.

Then he spoke.

THE BOOK

"This is for you."

He placed a book on the table. A book without wrapping. Without explanation. Without dedication.

Just a title: **THE MOUNTAIN.**

The book looked old and new at the same time, as if it had been read by many and yet had been waiting for her.

On the cover, a photograph of Mount Sinai outlined against a sky that seemed to burn.

Eliana stared without understanding.

"Why?" she asked, almost voiceless.

The man smiled— a calm smile, like someone who knows something he cannot yet say.

"Because you're going to need it."

And he left.

No tip. No card. No name.

Only the book.

Eliana picked it up with trembling hands. She didn't know why, but she felt the object had weight— not physical weight, but weight in the soul.

That night, in her small apartment, she opened the book.

And as she read, something inside her began to move.

It wasn't emotion.

It wasn't curiosity.

It was an echo— not from the book, but from a deeper place.

An ancient longing.

A wordless call.

A need she didn't know she had.

When she reached the last page, she closed the book with a sigh she couldn't explain. And she knew—without knowing how—that she had to go there.

To that mountain. To that desert. To that place where, according to the book, God had spoken.

She wasn't looking for religion.

She wasn't looking for miracles.

She wasn't looking for answers.

She was looking for air. For meaning. For a place where her soul could rest.

And so her journey began. Not toward Egypt. Not toward Sinai. Not toward a geographic destination.

But toward the place where her wound would be seen. Where her name would be spoken. Where her story would meet another story buried beneath centuries of sand.

Eliana didn't know it yet…

…but that book had already changed her destiny.

Because some destinies don't begin with decisions… they begin with callings.

THE SILENT DECISION-MAKER

During the days that followed, Eliana carried the book in her bag as if she were carrying something she wasn't sure was a memory, a sign, or a weight.

She opened it on the subway. She opened it during her break. She opened it before going to sleep.

Not to read it again, but to make sure it was still there.

There was something in those pages that wouldn't leave her alone. It wasn't guilt. It wasn't fear. It was something else— a gentle pull, as if an invisible hand were guiding her toward a place she did not yet know.

For years, Eliana had tried to heal her wounds on her own. Wounds born from the absence of a father and the harshness of a mother. Wounds from failed relationships. Wounds that made her feel belittled, stepped on, and treated like an object to be used.

Wounds that screamed for love, for attention, for worth… and all of them hidden beneath the appearance of a strong, fearless woman.

She had sought relief in yoga classes, guided meditations, spiritual retreats, therapy sessions, and religious groups that promised instant peace.

She tried breathing techniques, self-help books, counseling, rituals, silence, mantras.

But nothing touched what truly hurt. Nothing reached the bottom. Nothing managed to quiet the internal noise that haunted her even on her best days.

Her soul was tired.

Her body was tense, defensive, as if afraid of being hurt again. And her mind was suspicious of anything that sounded like hope.

But her spirit… her spirit reacted differently.

As she read The Mountain, something inside her lit up.

It wasn't emotion.

It wasn't illusion.

It was recognition—

as if her spirit understood a message her wounded soul could not yet decipher.

And for the first time in a long time, she felt she wasn't facing a technique, a method, or an empty promise.

She felt she was facing an opportunity— one that would not repeat itself. A door that would not open twice.

An invitation coming from a place higher than any therapy, deeper than any meditation, older than any religion.

And that mixture of intuition, need, and destiny produced an impulse born not of her mind or body, but of her spirit.

A silent yet firm impulse. An impulse that took hold of her entire being.

Unceremonious…

Without logic…

Without guarantees… Just obedience to something calling her from within.

And one night, as she listened to the noise of the city seeping through her apartment window, Eliana realized she had already made her decision. She didn't say it out loud. She didn't write it anywhere. She didn't share it with anyone.

She simply knew…

She knew she had to go. She knew she had to see that mountain. She knew she had to walk that desert. She knew she had to seek the God the book described with a closeness she had never felt.

And so, under that inexplicable certainty, she decided to travel.

She decided to buy the ticket. And without ceremony, without farewells, without explanations, she bought it.

A flight from New York to Cairo.

She chose to go to a place she didn't know, moved by a voice she hadn't heard, but which her spirit instantly recognized.

Eliana didn't know that this journey wouldn't take her to a mountain, but to an encounter.

She didn't know the desert was waiting for her.

She didn't know her name would be spoken.

She didn't know her wound would be seen.

She only knew she had to go.

And so, days later, she walked through John F. Kennedy Airport in New York with the book in her backpack…like someone carrying a map she did not yet know how to read.

THE FLIGHT

It wasn't the noise of the airport that exhausted her. Not the endless lines. Not the weight of the suitcase she dragged as if it carried inside it all the years she wanted to forget.

It was the silence.

That silence that settles in the chest when a woman has been hurt too many times and no longer knows whether she is fleeing… or simply walking so she won't remain in the same place.

Eliana wasn't looking at anyone. She wasn't searching for anything. She wasn't expecting anything.

She was simply moving forward.

The announcement for the flight to Cairo echoed through the loudspeakers, and she lifted her gaze as if obeying an ancient command—one she didn't understand, but felt.

It wasn't a tourist trip. Even though that's what she said when she requested vacation time. Even though that's what she wrote on the form. Even though that's what she told her mother, who didn't ask anything else.

It was a trip of escape. Of exhaustion. Of saturation. Of a life that had become too narrow for her soul.

Eliana handed over her passport. The agent looked at her for barely a second, long enough to confirm her name, her photo, her existence in a system.

But he didn't see her…

No one saw her…

…And that was why she was taking that flight.

As she walked through the tunnel toward the plane, she felt each step pulling her away from something she couldn't name. A pain. A man. A family. A story that had treated her as if she were expendable, a broken object easily replaced.

She sat by the window. Closed her eyes. Took a deep breath.

The plane took off… And as the city shrank beneath the clouds, Eliana felt—for the first time in a long time—that maybe, just maybe, she was heading toward a place where pain could not reach her.

She didn't know that place wasn't in Egypt. Not in Saint Catherine. Not even in the desert.

That place was buried beneath centuries of sand. Waiting for her. Waiting for her hands. Waiting for her wound. Waiting for her name.

CAIRO AIRPORT

Eliana didn't sleep during the flight. Not because she couldn't, but because she didn't want to close her eyes. When you've been hurt too many times, closing your eyes feels like a risk.

She looked out the window as the plane descended. The desert appeared first as a golden whisper, then as an immensity that seemed to have no end— an ancient land, a land that didn't ask permission to exist.

When the plane touched down, Eliana felt a small tremor in her chest. It wasn't fear. It was something deeper— as if a part of her already knew this trip wasn't an escape, but an encounter.

Cairo Airport greeted her with dry heat and a murmur of voices in languages she didn't understand.

People walked quickly, as if everyone knew exactly where they were going.

She didn't.

Eliana moved forward with her backpack on her shoulder, feeling each step make her more foreign. Smaller. More alone.

But also lighter.

She had left behind a life that treated her as if she were invisible. Here, in this unknown land, no one knew who she was. No one knew what she had lived. No one knew what she had lost.

And for an instant, that was a relief.

THE ROAD TO SAINT CATHERINE

Eliana left Cairo Airport with the book in her backpack, as if she were carrying a borrowed heart she did not yet know how to use.

The heat wrapped around her immediately— a dry, ancient heat, as if the air had been stored in clay jars for centuries and had just now been released.

She took a taxi to the bus station.

The driver spoke quickly, mixing Arabic with English, his cheerful tone contrasting with the silence inside Eliana.

She looked out the window.

The city was a beautiful chaos: makeshift markets, children running, women in colorful scarves, men smoking on street corners, cars moving as if guided by intuition rather than rules.

THE BOOK

Everything was noise. Everything was life. Everything was too much.

And yet, for the first time in a long time, Eliana felt she wasn't running away… She was arriving.

The bus to Saint Catherine left before noon, when the sun was already falling vertically over the city. Eliana sat by the window, as if she needed to witness every mile separating her from her past.

The desert appeared quickly, as if it had been waiting behind the last street— an immense, golden, silent expanse breathing with its own rhythm. And in the distance, the Red Sea shimmered with a light her soul longed for.

Eliana rested her forehead against the hot glass… The movement of the bus was almost hypnotic, rocking her toward a dream she didn't dare imagine.

The book lay on her lap. She opened it without reading—just to feel it. To remember that this object had been the beginning of everything.

The road wound through reddish, sharp, ancient mountains, as if carved by invisible hands. The sky was clear, without a single cloud, as if the day wanted to reveal everything without hiding anything.

Eliana took a deep breath… She felt something she hadn't felt in years: expectation.

She didn't know what she was looking for. She didn't know what she would find. She didn't know what awaited her.

But for the first time, she wasn't afraid…

The desert was calling her…

…And she was answering.

THE ACCIDENT

The bus moved along the Sinai Highway like a metal serpent sliding through reddish mountains. The midday sun fell vertically sharp, merciless, leaving no shadows to hide in.

Eliana had been watching the desert for more than an hour.

There was something hypnotic about that immense landscape, as if each dune held a secret and each mountain stood as a silent guardian.

And in the distance, she saw a bird. A bird gliding through the air, mastering the wind. A bird shining under the sun.

As the bus advanced, the bird drew closer, flying as if chasing the vehicle, as if coming to meet it, as if it were an old friend.

For a moment, Eliana thought it would strike the bus. But it didn't. It passed by… and disappeared.

The driver was talking to another passenger in Arabic, laughing at something Eliana didn't understand. The engine vibrated with a steady, almost comforting rhythm.

Until it didn't.

First came a strange sound, a thud, as if something had burst beneath the bus. Then a violent pull to the right.

Eliana grabbed the seat.

The driver shouted something no one could understand.

The bus began to shake, not like a machine losing control, but like a wounded animal trying to stay upright.

Eliana felt her heart rise to her throat.

The desert rushed past the window—fast, too fast.

The driver fought the steering wheel. The bus skidded on gravel. A metallic screech tore through the air.

And then—everything stopped.

No explosion. No rollover. No screams… Just a dry, cutting silence, as if the desert had swallowed the sound.

Eliana opened her eyes.

The bus was tilted, one tire buried in the sand. The engine smoked. Passengers murmured, confused, but unharmed.

The driver got out first, muttering, shaking his head. He looked at the shredded tire, then at the empty road.

"No one comes here," he said in broken English.

"We wait."

Eliana stepped off the bus.

The heat wrapped around her like a rough embrace. The sun hammered the sand, which shone like ground glass.

No shade.

No wind.

Nothing… Only desert.

The other passengers stayed near the bus, searching for signal on their phones, finding nothing but silence.

Eliana walked a few steps away. She didn't know why. She didn't know what she was looking for.

She just felt she had to walk.

The desert called her, not with words, not with voices, but with a deep sensation, as if something beneath the sand were breathing.

THE BOOK

She walked a few more meters. The sun burned the back of her neck. The air was so dry it felt like it could cut.

And then, without thinking, without understanding, without planning…

…she began to dig.

Not in desperation. Not in panic. Not with the intention of dying.

But with a strange mixture of exhaustion and devotion, like someone opening a hole to leave behind something they can no longer carry.

The sand was hot, soft, light, slipping through her fingers like ancient dust.

She dug… And dug… And dug.

Until her hands touched something that wasn't sand. Something hard. Something cold. Something that did not belong to the desert.

Eliana froze. Her heart pounded in her ears. She brushed the sand away carefully.

And there it was.

A sealed clay cylinder. Old. Cracked. Covered in centuries of silence.

A parchment. A buried book. A message waiting for her.

Eliana held it in her trembling hands. The sun illuminated the object as if it had been saving it for that exact moment.

And without knowing it, without understanding it, without even imagining it, she had found the story that would change her life… the story of a woman who, like her, had been seen in her affliction.

THE PARCHMENT OPENS

Eliana held the clay cylinder as if afraid it would crumble at her touch. The seal was cracked but still firm, as if it had waited centuries only to open in that instant.

Carefully, she broke it.

An ancient scent rose from within, dust, oil, time. A chill ran down her arms. It wasn't fear.

It was recognition, as if something inside her knew this object wasn't foreign, but familiar.

She pulled out the scroll.

The texture was rough yet warm. The dark ink, still alive. The letters seemed to breathe, as if they had not been written, but spoken.

Eliana unrolled it a little more. The desert sun illuminated the first line. A cool breeze brushed her face.

She read in silence.

And then, without noticing, without feeling the transition, the voice speaking was no longer hers.

It was another.

An ancient voice.

A weary voice.

A wise voice.

A voice that had waited centuries to be heard.

The desert was still that afternoon, as if it had chosen to rest with her.

And then…

…a buried story…

….began to speak.

Chapter 2

"THE PARCHMENT"

The Messenger's Writing for a Woman

The writing began like this…

The desert was still that afternoon, as if it had decided to rest by embracing time in its fullness.

The sunlight did not hurt or burn; it simply lay upon the sand, spreading in a soft glow that demanded nothing. It was a mature light, like that of an old man who no longer needs to prove his strength.

The wind moved slowly among the tents scattered across the plain, barely stirring the thick fabrics that formed the camp. Around them, a few tall palm trees swayed in a gentle rhythm, as if they too were breathing.

A faint aroma of dried dates and warm milk drifted through the air, mingling with the soft murmur of water falling into the nearby well.

That place—lost somewhere in the northern Arabian Peninsula—was a refuge.

A small oasis built by nomadic hands, sustained by the patience of the desert and the faithfulness of water.

The camels rested in the shade, chewing calmly, as if they knew the secret of eternal stillness.

Everything was peaceful.

In the distance, the boys—twelve tall, agile young men with steady eyes—moved around the camp as if they were part of the landscape.

They did not run.

They did not shout.

They simply existed—secure, strong, confident— as if they had been born knowing the world belonged to them. There was something in their walk that announced destiny, as if each one carried on his shoulders the seed of a future tribe, a people not yet named.

Among them, a man of imposing presence watched in silence.

Ishmael.

His shadow was long, but his gaze was calm.

He had learned to protect without violence, to watch without fear, to hold without crushing. His life had been hard, but his heart was no longer hardened.

And at the center of it all—like the trunk of a tree that has survived every season—was her.

Hagar.

Sitting beneath the wide shade of a tamarisk tree, her hands resting on her lap, her eyes lost in a horizon only she could see. Her face bore wrinkles, yes— but they were wrinkles of history, not of pain. Wrinkles of one who has cried, but also of one who has laughed. Wrinkles of one who has been wounded, but also of one who has been healed.

There was abundance in the camp:

Meat hanging to dry.

Full wineskins.

Baskets of dates.

Young laughter.

Old silences.

Everything in balance… Everything in harmony… Everything at that exact point where life no longer weighs, but is cherished.

Hagar took a deep breath.

The desert air entered her chest like an old friend. There was no hurry in her breathing. No shadow in her soul.

Only gratitude.

Only rest.

Only the calm certainty of someone who once received a seed… and now rests beneath the shade of the tree that grew from it.

That was when she saw it.

The well.

HER OLD FRIEND'S CRACK

The same well that had accompanied her family for years.

The same well that had sustained the lives of her children and her children's children.

The same well that had witnessed long nights and new mornings.

The same well she had seen before.

But that afternoon, something different caught her attention.

A crack…

Small…

Thin…

Barely visible…

But there.

A dark line on the stone.

A wound along the edge.

A fissure that had not been there yesterday.

Hagar slowly rose and walked toward the well.

When she placed her hand on the warm stone, she did not do it in haste or with concern… She did it with love.

The stone was warm, but deep inside the well there was a soft echo— like an ancient sigh rising from the water.

The sun fell at an angle that left a golden reflection on the surface, as if the well kept light inside it.

Her fingers traced the crack as tenderly as a mother touches the face of a sleeping child.

It was a soft, intimate, almost reverent touch.

As if the well were someone.

As if it were breathing.

As if it guarded an ancient secret only she could understand.

And as her fingers followed the line of the crack, something flowed within her.

Not pain.

Not bitter nostalgia.

But a mixture of tenderness, understanding, care, sustenance, affection… love.

Each touch of her fingers released a tear down her face. But it was not a tear of suffering. It was a contemplative tear— a tear born from deep love for the one thing that had sustained her when no one else did.

The well… The crack.

Her hand… Her tear.

And there, in that instant suspended between light and shadow, between the present and the past… Hagar began to remember her story.

HAGAR SPEAKS TO THE WELL

My well…

…how many times have I touched you like this, with the same tenderness that is reborn in my hands today.

Your stone is warm, as if you still hold the heat of all the lives you have sustained.

And as my fingers trace this crevice, I feel as though I am touching more than stone… I feel as though I am touching memory.

This crack… this small wound that time has opened along your edge… it speaks to me of my own time.

Just as you begin to break with the passing years, I too feel my days bending toward their twilight.

My time to leave is approaching, and before I go… I want to tell you something I never told you.

Because when I first met you, I was devastated.

Broken.

Full of cracks I did not know how to name.

You witnessed my tears, my fear, my loneliness. But I never dared to tell you my whole story.

I had no words…

I had no strength…

I had no voice…

But today I do.

Today I can speak to you without trembling.

Today I can touch you without breaking.

Today I can look at you without falling into the abyss that once swallowed me.

And I want to tell you my story—not from sadness, but from this contemplation that is born when one understands that an encounter can transform any destiny.

Because that is what happened to me.

An encounter…

An encounter can heal wounds that seemed eternal.

An encounter can ease a pain that once had no name.

An encounter can ignite hope where there was only dust.

An encounter can teach you to live, to dream, to strive, to rise, to believe that the impossible can happen…

The Messenger told me one day…

He spoke to me of a future I could not imagine.

He spoke to me of a son who would be strong.

He spoke to me of a nation that would be born from my womb.

He spoke to me of life when all I saw was death.

And today…

from that future which is now my present, from this abundance that was once only a promise, from this peace that was once a desert…

I want to tell you everything.

Chapter 3

"THE GIRL"

The Hollows in My Soul That Shaped Me

Before I tell you what I lived on this earth, my well… before I tell you about Abraham, Sarah, the desert, and the Messenger… I want to take you further back.

To a time I do not remember, but that belongs to me. A time that was told to me, yet marked my soul before I even knew I had one.

I was born far from here.

Very far.

Beyond the great river, in lands my feet never touched again.

My parents were not Egyptians…

They were foreigners, like me.

They were wanderers, like me.

They were landless souls, as I was for so many years.

My father…

I have not a single memory of him.

Not his voice. Not his face.

Not his scent.

Nothing.

Only a gap— a hollow so vast that even as an old woman, I still feel it open inside me when I speak his name.

That emptiness was my cradle.

My inheritance.

My first wound.

All I have are the words my mother repeated when sadness overtook her.

She told me he dreamed of me before I was born.

That he spoke of me as if he had already seen me.

That he said I would be great, strong, important— like a queen among the peoples.

My mother mocked him.

She told him to stop speaking nonsense, that life did not give greatness to the poor, that dreams did not feed anyone.

But he insisted.

He insisted with a faith I now understand—a faith that was not his, but the faith of the God who saw me by the well.

My father died before I could walk.

He died in an invasion, in one of those wars between kings that destroy homes without asking names.

My mother fled with me in her arms, running through smoke, through screams, through blood I do not remember— but that she could never forget.

That is why she called me Hagar.

"Flight."

"Foreigner."

"Fugitive."

That was my name before I knew how to speak. That was my destiny before I knew how to live.

I grew up with a void as large as the dream my father had for me. A hollow I did not know how to name, but that I felt in my chest— like a crack opening before life even begins.

My mother… she had her own crack. A crack made of pain, of bitterness, of unanswered questions.

She complained about fate, about the gods, about luck, about life.

I listened in silence… always in silence.

Since childhood, I learned to be silent.

To swallow.

To observe.

To feel without speaking.

To suffer without noise.

To exist without taking up space.

Because when a girl grows up with a hole that big… she learns to make herself small so no one notices it.

CHILDHOOD IN EGYPT

When we arrived in Egypt, I was only a child.

I didn't understand the language, I didn't know the customs, I didn't know anything about the world.

All I knew was that my mother cried at night, and that I had no father to hold me when fear woke me.

Egypt was a strange place for me. There was so much movement… so much life… so much noise… so much greatness mixed with misery.

I saw men in simple robes, but I also saw others who looked like gods—their painted eyes, their necks covered in gold, their steps firm, as if the earth itself belonged to them.

I grew up seeing small houses like ours, and palaces so large they seemed to touch the sky.

And although I lived in a humble house, my heart always rose toward the palaces. Not because I desired them… but because they were the only thing that reminded me of my father.

My mother told me he dreamed of seeing me grown, strong, important.

That he spoke of me as if I were already a queen.

And although I had no memory of him— no face, no voice, no embrace— I clung to his dream.

That dream was the only thing I had from him. The only thing that belonged to me. The only thing that held me up when life hurt too much.

Because when I saw other families— a father, a mother, children laughing— something inside me broke.

THE GIRL

I didn't have that…

I never had it…

My father's absence was an immense hollow, a void as great as the dream he had for me.

And my mother… my mother could not fill that void.

She herself was broken. Loss had made her bitter, sad, distrustful of fate. She complained about everything—everyone—life itself.

And I… I learned to be silent.

Since childhood, I learned to swallow my tears, to hide my questions, to keep my fears tucked away.

I learned to observe in silence, to feel without speaking, to suffer without noise.

But I also learned to shine.

Not because of the reality of my life, but because of the beauty of my father's dream.

That dream became my refuge, my shelter, my strength. And the more I clung to it, the more something inside me began to change.

My face began to brighten.

My gaze grew steady.

My brown skin glowed in the sun.

My light eyes drew attention without my seeking it.

My straight hair danced in the wind as if it had a life of its own.

It was a strange mixture—grace covering misfortune, light rising from the crack, beauty springing from pain.

And that light… that light that was not mine, but the dream my father left in me… began to draw attention.

Pharaoh's captains saw me. They watched me in silence. And one day, without warning,

I was taken to serve in the palaces.

But that… that is another story.

THE JOY OF BEING CHOSEN

The day they announced that some young women would be recruited to serve in Pharaoh's palaces, my heart almost leapt out of my chest.

Not all were chosen.

Not all had that opportunity.

And when I heard my name, I felt my father's dream breathe inside me.

I ran home with a joy too big for my steps.

My mother was grinding grain, as always, with that tired gesture that never left her.

I burst in, almost out of breath.

"Mother!" I said. "Mother, I've been chosen!"

She looked up, surprised, and asked:

"Chosen for what?"

I answered with all the enthusiasm and joy in my soul: "To serve in the palaces—in Pharaoh's palaces!"

My voice trembled, but not from fear.

It trembled with hope.

"Mother," I said, smiling from the deepest part of me, "my father was right…"

Instantly she dropped the millstone.

The sound was dry, harsh—like a blow against the ground.

She looked at me with a mixture of anger and sorrow and asked:

"What are you saying, Hagar?"

Softly, I replied:

"He knew, Mother… He knew I would be important. How did he know? How could he see it?"

My mother closed her eyes.

Her breathing grew heavy.

And then, in a broken voice, she told me something she had never said before.

"Your father," she whispered, "once said he met a strange man. A man who did not seem of this world. They called him the Messenger."

And that man told him he would have a daughter—a daughter who would be great, important, destined for something he could not understand.

Her words faltered…

Her eyes filled with tears…

And suddenly, as if pain were piercing her, she cried out:

"Your father was mad, Hagar!

Mad!

He spoke nonsense.

And now you—you're starting to talk just like him.

Where do you get such madness?

Where do you get so much enthusiasm?"

Her words were harsh— stones thrown at my chest. But they did not hurt me. Not that day.

Because while she spoke, I was carefully folding my clothes—the little I had—arranging them with a joy I could not hide.

My heart was full.

Full of light.

Full of future.

Full of my father's dream.

I did not see madness… I saw destiny.

THE GIRL

As my mother wept for what she had lost, I smiled for what was coming.

Because for the first time in my life…

I saw myself as great.

I saw myself as important.

I saw myself walking among marble columns, beneath golden lamps, among voices speaking languages I did not yet know.

My young heart pounded—with the strength only those who dream without fear possess, with the energy born when hope is greater than the wound.

And so, with my few belongings wrapped in a cloak, with my father's dream burning in my chest, and with my mother's gaze lost in tears…

I prepared to enter Pharaoh's palaces.

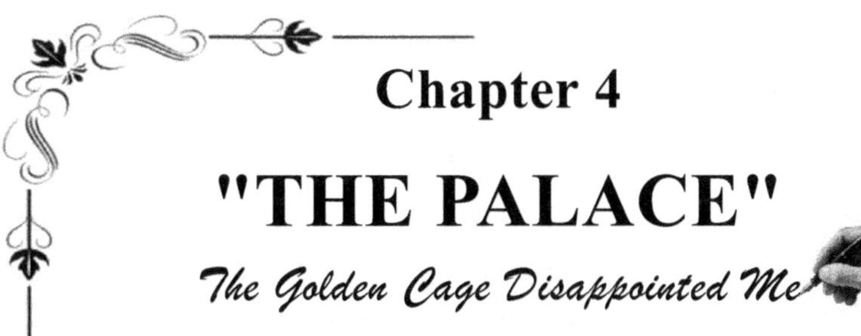

Chapter 4

"THE PALACE"

The Golden Cage Disappointed Me

When I first walked through the palace gates, I felt as if my feet were no longer touching the ground.

Everything was larger than anything my imagination had ever dared to dream.

Huge columns. Walls painted in colors I had never seen. Statues that seemed alive. And a solemn silence that made every step echo as if it mattered.

I was full of expectations.

Full of energy.

Full of that intense joy only the young possess—those who believe destiny is calling them by name.

But the first thing they did was take everything from me.

My clothes.

My cloak.

My small bundle of belongings.

My worn fabrics.

My old sandals.

Everything that had been mine… everything that had been my life… they discarded without looking at me twice.

"You won't use any of that here," they told me.

Then they took me to a purification room. I will never forget that moment.

I froze when I saw the women approaching. I was not used to anyone seeing my nakedness. My body had always been mine—covered, protected, hidden.

But they did not look at me with judgment.

They looked at me as if I were a vessel to be cleansed, as if my skin were clay being prepared for a new purpose.

They bathed me.

They washed my hair.

They immersed me in warm waters filled with aromatic flowers.

The water made a soft sound as it fell against the stone—an ancient murmur. The flowers released a sweet, heavy fragrance, and my fingers glided over oils that left my skin so soft it no longer felt like my own.

I spent hours there, soaking, and for the first time I discovered that there were scents other than sun and earth.

My fragrance changed… My skin changed… My breathing changed.

I no longer smelled of desert… I no longer smelled of flight… I no longer smelled of poverty.

I smelled of sweet flowers, of perfumed oils—of something I had never known.

Then they dressed me in fabrics my fingers could not comprehend, soft, light and almost alive.

I spent hours touching them, smelling them, feeling them slide over my skin like water.

They taught me how to walk.

How to sit.

How to stand.

How to bow.

How to dance.

How to speak softly.

How to look without lowering my eyes.

How to move my hands as if they were part of a music I had not yet learned to hear.

They were sculpting me.

Molding me.

Transforming me.

And I was happy—happy because every gesture, every perfume, every fabric, every instruction told me that my father's dream was real.

He had seen it.

He had spoken it.

He had believed it.

And I… I was living what he dreamed.

The food changed as well.

I had been used to eating only what was necessary—what I could.

But there… there I discovered flavors that seemed invented by the gods: sweet dates, soft breads, spiced meats, fruits that looked like jewels.

It was no longer just smelling fragrances. No longer just touching silks. Now it was tasting delicacies I had never imagined.

My classes began too. Priests and magicians taught us about the gods of Egypt. There were many—too many. Each with its story, its temple, its power.

And silently, I asked myself:

Which of all these gods is the greatest?

Which one did my father see?

Which one spoke to him?

What sustains my destiny?

Will He ever speak to me?

Or do the gods not speak to people like me?

These were questions I kept inside, as I always had—questions no one heard, but that followed me like a soft shadow.

Years passed like this.

THE PALACE

Years of learning, of perfumes, of fabrics, of banquets, of rituals, of teachings, of illusions.

And in the midst of those years… I learned that my mother had died.

Something inside me went out—like a lamp running out of oil. I did not cry. I could not. The pain was so deep it could not rise to the surface.

I was not allowed to attend her funeral. I could no longer mix with ordinary people, much less with foreigners.

I belonged to the palace now—to its world, to its rules.

I swallowed hard…and kept silent.

Once again.

First it had been my father's absence. Now it was my mother's. The palace became my home. My family. My world. My gods. My identity.

But over time… when everything stopped being new, when perfumes no longer surprised me, when fabrics no longer amazed me, when banquets became routine… something inside me began to empty.

A void I could not explain.

A void without a name.

A void that grew in silence.

Because my father's words—those words that spoke of greatness—were larger than anything I was living.

And one day, looking into the bronze mirror, I whispered to myself:

This is not greatness.

I am only a refined slave.

A perfumed slave.

An educated slave.

A slave who eats well and dresses well…

…but still a slave.

SARAI'S ARRIVAL AT THE PALACE

It had been several years since I entered the palace.

Years of perfumes, soft fabrics, banquets, teachings, rituals.

Years in which I had been molded like a fine vessel—but inside… inside I was still the girl who had learned to be silent.

I served the queen with dedication.

I watched her in silence as she walked with the confidence of one who is a wife, who is a mother, who belongs.

And every time I assisted her, something inside me shrank.

Because I could not have a husband… Nor children… Nor a home… Nor even a proper name.

I was a refined slave. A perfumed slave. An educated slave. But a slave nonetheless.

And secretly… when no one saw me… I cried.

I spoke to myself, as I had done since childhood:

“Are you foolish, Hagar?

Believing in other people's dreams?

Believing the words of a man you don't even remember?

Your mother was right…"

But there was another voice inside me. A small voice—yet firm. A voice that had always accompanied me, since before Egypt, since before the palace.

"This is not your father's dream… but this is the road to it. I do not know which of these gods will act… but what he saw—what was announced to him—will be fulfilled."

I lived between two voices… Between two worlds… Between two truths.

Between disappointment and encouragement.

Between joy and sadness.

Between lies and hope.

Between unbelief and faith.

And while my heart debated with itself, I heard shouting at the back of the palace.

Hurried steps.

Orders.

Guards running.

Something was happening.

THE PALACE

I went out to see, with the discretion we had been taught. One of my companions approached, breathless.

“The captain has found a very beautiful woman for Pharaoh,” she said.

“A foreigner.

They say she comes from the other side of the river…”

My heart stopped for a moment.

“Will they train her like us?” I asked.

She shook her head.

“No. She will not be taken as a slave. She is being brought for something higher. Superior.”

That word fell on me like a stone.

Amid the sound of guards’ boots, amid the murmurs in the corridors, amid the hurried movement of the palace… my heart broke.

I did not feel envy… Nor anger… Nor jealousy.

I did not know her. I did not know her name. I had not seen her face. But it was impossible not to feel something inside me fracture.

A deep, silent, sharp disillusionment—as if I had been climbing a mountain for years and suddenly… someone pushed me into the valley.

The entire castle I had built in my heart began to crumble.

Another woman more beautiful than me. For a position higher than mine.

So… all this time, had I been deceiving myself?

And that emotion—that clawed disappointment—dragged me into other emotions I thought I had buried:

My father's absence.

My mother's absence.

My fugitive name.

My rootless origin.

My life of escape.

My identity as a perfumed slave.

And there, in the midst of the palace's splendor, surrounded by gold, perfumes, soft fabrics, towering columns…

…I felt emptier than ever.

MY FIRST MEETING WITH SARAI

I had entered an emotional place I had always avoided.

A dark place.

A place I had known since childhood, but from which I had always fled.

I felt like a failure.

Frustrated.

As if my destiny were to suffer—as if life itself were saying to me:

"This is who you are. This is who you will always be."

And for the first time… I began to believe it. The evidence was there—clear, cold, sharp.

The queen had a husband. She had children. She had a place. She had a name.

I had none of that.

Nor could I ever have it.

I was not allowed to dream of it.

And secretly, I cried…

I cried like I did as a child.

I cried like when I lost my father.

I cried like when I lost my mother.

I cried like when I realized the palace was not a home, but a perfumed cage.

As I sobbed silently, I was summoned.

My mistress.

Her voice firm, emotionless.

"Hagar, come. You will prepare the foreigner."

That phrase… it was the straw that broke the camel's back.

A fire rose in my chest.

I wanted to scream.

I wanted to flee.

I wanted to break something.

I wanted to break down.

But I restrained myself. As always. As all my life.

I fell silent.

I swallowed.

I breathed.

And I walked.

As I made my way to the room where the woman waited, I prepared myself to accept what I believed was the truth:

"My father was mad."

"He was hallucinating."

"The gods don't speak to people like him."

"Much less to someone like me."

"I have lived deceived."

"I believed in a dream that was never mine."

Every step was a renunciation. Every breath a defeat. Every thought another stone on my chest.

THE PALACE

I reached the room. I entered with learned courtesy, with the submission I had been taught, with a broken heart.

And there she was…

The foreign woman. The most beautiful woman. The woman destined for something higher.

Sarai.

I bathed her as they had bathed me.

I purified her as they had purified me.

I prepared her as they had prepared me.

But she did not understand my words. She spoke another language. Her hands trembled. Her eyes were full of fear.

And yet, something about her felt familiar—as if our wounds recognized each other before our voices ever could.

She did not know why I was crying.

I did not know why she was trembling.

We could not speak.

But we looked at one another…

Me, with a broken heart… She, with her heart in danger.

Me, with old wounds… She, with a husband she might lose.

Me, with a destiny crumbling… She, with a destiny being taken from her.

Days passed.

THE PALACE

I continued preparing her. And I noticed something: The fragrances they gave her were superior. The fabrics finer. The rituals longer. The care more delicate.

She would not be a slave… She would be something more.

And in my days of nostalgia, when I no longer had the strength to cry, something happened that I had never seen.

The palace was invaded by plagues.

Horrendous plagues.

Creatures entering through windows, falling from ceilings, crawling into food.

Plagues that stole sleep.

The sound was unbearable—a living, insistent buzzing, as if thousands of wings beat against the palace walls. Shadows moved in the corners, and the air smelled of dampness and fear.

It was as if darkness had come to live with us.

And I thought:

"That is my heart. Full of things that should not be there. Full of shadows. Full of death."

I whispered to myself, with sad sarcasm:

"Well… at least I smell good. I smell good and dress well… for a slave."

The priests performed rituals.

They invoked all their gods.

But nothing changed.

It seemed their gods were on vacation. Or deaf. Or dead.

Then I heard the guards' boots.

Again.

Running.

Urgent.

Something was happening.

A companion approached me and whispered:

"That woman you've been preparing… she is married."

"Married?" I asked.

She nodded: "Yes. And they are Hebrews."

"Who are they?" I Asked again.

She lowered her voice: "Filthy people. An abomination to us and to our gods."

A blow struck my stomach. Inwardly, I thought…

"Then I have been preparing a filthy woman?

Will I now be rejected by the gods as well?"

She continued telling me:

"They went to fetch her husband. Pharaoh wants to speak with him."

"They will probably kill him," I said. "For lying."

"No," she answered. "If that man's god is the one who brought these plagues… if they kill him, that god will kill us all."

I stood motionless.

"So… is that man's god stronger than all our gods combined?"

She did not answer. They called her away. She left.

And I remained silent. Dismayed. Full of questions. Full of new cracks.

For a moment, my depression paused. And I entered a state I did not know: search.

I wanted answers.

I needed answers.

A few minutes passed… The plagues vanished. Just like that. Suddenly.

Then I heard footsteps.

Boots.

Sandals.

Voices.

They were approaching my door.

I stepped back.

One step.

Another.

Another.

And suddenly, the door opened.

"Prepare the foreigner," the guard ordered.

"She is leaving. And you are going with her."

I was stunned.

I felt nothing.

Not joy.

Not sadness.

Not fear.

Only emptiness. A deep void. A hollowness that froze me.

A guard grabbed my arm.

"Move. Hurry. We don't want trouble with that god. You go with them. Now."

And so… once again…

I fled.

THE PALACE

My name reached me again.

Hagar — the fugitive.

As if destiny reminded me who I was every time I tried to forget.

But this time, not by my legs.

Not by my will.

Not by my choice.

But by force.

Torn away.

Banished.

Banished from a place that was never mine.

Exiled without a father.

Without a mother.

Without a dream.

Without a palace.

Without fragrance.

Without identity.

I was returning to the sun.

Returning to the earth.

Returning to poverty.

But worse than before… because now I was a slave to a family considered unclean.

And I thought:

"I thought I had already hit rock bottom. But there is always a deeper bottom for the one destined to lose."

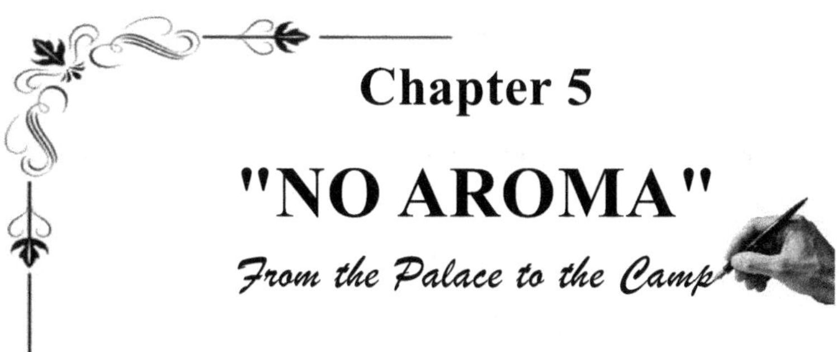

Chapter 5

"NO AROMA"

From the Palace to the Camp

As I left the palace, I felt my soul crack like a glass jar thrown against the ground.

The pieces of my heart scattered inside me—sharp, cold, impossible to gather.

My silence… that silence I had learned since childhood… that silence that had been my refuge and my prison… that day it earned a doctorate.

I did not complain.

I did not protest.

I did not scream.

I had grown up without parental protection. I had never had a man to defend me. Never had an embrace that said, "I am with you." So I did not know how to rebel. I did not know how to demand. I did not know how to say "no."

It was easier to be submissive than to raise my voice. Easier to be silent than to confront. Easier to obey than to exist.

I was afraid…

I was insecure…

…My soul was in pieces.

And then… I saw him.

Abram.

For a moment, I felt something unfamiliar—a mixture of respect, fear, curiosity…and something else I could not name.

That man carried a distinct aura. A steady energy. A presence that imposed itself without effort.

He looked like a bear. He looked like a lion. He looked like a creature born to rule the wilderness without asking permission.

There was something in him—something even Pharaoh had recognized.

Because Pharaoh had given him gifts. Many. Too many.

And among those gifts… was me.

I was part of the loot. Part of the payment. Part of the fear.

As we walked away from Egypt, I tried to find something positive—as I always did.

"If Pharaoh and his priests fear this man's God… then that God is stronger than all the ones I knew."

Maybe… maybe one day I could learn their language. Maybe one day I could hear them speak of that God. Maybe… maybe that God would see me too.

We walked… And walked… And walked.

And just as Egypt faded behind me, I tried to push my emotions away. Tried to hide them. Bury them. Lock them in some corner of my heart where they would not interfere.

But the dispossession was inevitable.

My perfume dissipated. My clothes tore. The sweet scent of oils faded day after day until only the harsh smell of sweat and sand remained. It was as if my skin slowly forgot that it had once been touched by flowers.

They gave me rough fabrics—like the ones I wore when I lived with my mother. My skin, once softened by ointments, grew hardened again by sun and sand.

I smelled the earth again.

I smelled the sun again.

I smelled of flight again.

And in that ancient, harsh scent, I recognized my mother's shadow—her absence still there, a hollow that never closed.

Day after day… Week after week… Month after month.

As time passed, I learned their language. I learned to cook as they cooked. To walk as they walked. To live as they lived.

They were many—more than three hundred people.

Sometimes, in the silent nights of the camp, I thought I still heard the hum of the plagues that had invaded the palace—a sound stuck in my ears like a memory that refused to leave.

But they lived in peace. A peace I had never seen in Egypt. A peace that did not depend on perfumes or palaces.

And I noticed something strange… Abram and Sarai had no children.

And every time I saw her walk among the tents, something about her unsettled me. It was not beauty. It was not authority. It was an invisible thread—as if her story and mine were tied together, though I did not yet know how.

How strange, I thought.

Such a large people… and no children.

And so the years passed. I grew accustomed to their way of life. There were no marble columns. No banquets. No silks. No beauty rituals.

But there was peace.

And though I was still a slave… I did not feel like one.

My soul, once crushed, began to find a small comfort. A gentle calm. A new breath.

For the first time since leaving the palace, I felt I could exist without breaking.

But even in that calm, my name continued to haunt me. Hagar — the fugitive. As if every step I took reminded me that I was always running from something… or toward something I did not yet understand.

THE ROAD WITH FOREIGNERS

When we left Egypt, I wasn't just leaving a country behind. I was leaving behind everything I understood.

In Egypt, since childhood, I had been taught to recognize hierarchies—to know who was who, to identify ranks, titles, lineages, symbols, to understand my place… always low, always small, always silent.

But in this new group… everything was different.

NO AROMA

There were no columns. No thrones. No priests in golden masks. No soldiers with spears. No scribes taking notes.

There were only tents. Animals. Dust. And a man who walked ahead as if he knew exactly where he was going, even though the road was nothing but sand.

That man was Abram.

He needed no crown. No escort. No raised voice. His authority was silent— like a mountain that does not ask permission to exist.

Sarai walked beside him. She did not speak much, but her presence was firm, as if she carried within her a secret I could not yet understand.

Behind them I saw a young man. At first I thought he was Abram's son—he had the age, the strength, the posture. But soon I learned he was not a son… but a nephew. And that nephew already had a wife. And children.

And then something struck me inside.

Abram had no children. Not one. Not even a small child running between the tents.

But he had shepherds. Many. And his nephew had many too. It was as if they were both leaders of something I could not grasp.

And there… that's when my mind began to compare.

In Egypt, a man without children was a man without a future—a man without inheritance, without a name, without continuity.

But this man… this Abram… he walked as if he carried a destiny greater than all the children of the world combined.

And I understood nothing.

As I walked behind them, my thoughts tangled with my memories. I remembered my father—his voice telling me I would be great, that I would be important, that I would reach high places.

I remembered my mother laughing at him, calling him mad, telling me not to believe in dreams, that life was hard, that I was just a poor girl destined to serve.

And there, in the middle of the desert, among foreigners, homeless, aimless, without identity… I felt my father's words melt inside me like water slipping through my fingers.

I lost my balance… I grew discouraged… I sank.

I thought:

"I am nothing. I will be nothing. My father was wrong. My life has no destiny."

And while everyone moved forward, I walked with my body… but my soul stayed behind—crawling, trying not to break more than it already had.

THE SEPARATION OF ABRAM AND LOT

As the days passed, I began to notice something strange among the shepherds. It wasn't an open fight, but a tension—hard looks, whispers, small arguments growing like embers hidden beneath the sand.

Abram's and Lot's flocks were too many.

Too many animals.

Too many men.

Too much shared land.

NO AROMA

In Egypt, when conflict arose, Pharaoh imposed his will—a gesture, an order, a punishment—and everything aligned.

But here… here I saw something I had never seen.

Abram called Lot. Not as a superior calls an inferior, but as a man calls someone he loves.

They climbed to a high place together. I followed from a distance, as I always did—not out of curiosity, but because I needed to understand this new world that had no columns, no temples, no statues.

From above, the valley stretched out like a blanket of green—beautiful, fertile, full of life.

And then I heard Abram say something that took my breath away:

"If you go to the left, I will go to the right. If you go to the right, I will go to the left."

I froze.

I didn't understand.

The leader—the man everyone followed, the one with more shepherds, more cattle, more authority—was giving Lot the first choice? The best land?

In Egypt, that would never have happened. Never.

Pharaoh always took the best. Always… And the rest received the leftovers.

But Abram… Abram acted as if his heart was larger than his territory—as if loving were more important than possessing.

And I… I didn't know what to do with that.

NO AROMA

Lot looked over the valley. I saw it in his eyes—he wanted the best, the greenest, the most fertile, the easiest.

And Abram let him choose. No anger. No complaint. No fear.

When Lot left with his shepherds, Abram remained alone at the top. And then he did something that baffled me even more.

He knelt.

He bowed.

He prostrated himself.

There was no statue. No idol. No carved figure. No stone altar like in Egypt.

Only him. The soil. And a God I could not see.

I watched from afar—his bent body, his face against the earth, his hands open, his voice low, as if speaking to someone who was there… even though I saw no one.

And something inside me broke.

For as I watched Abram love Lot unconditionally… as I watched Abram worship an invisible God… as I watched Abram trust without clinging… I remembered my life.

I remembered that I had never known a love like that—not from a father, not from a mother, not from anyone.

I remembered that in Egypt, animals received more affection than I did—horses were stroked, dogs were spoken to, cats were given milk… and I… I was just a shadow that served.

While Abram bowed to his God, I bowed to my sorrow. I felt myself falling—descending into myself—my soul sinking into a bottomless pit.

I thought:

"Maybe this is my destiny. To be invisible. To be used. To be handed over like an object. To be less than an animal. To be a woman without love."

And while Abram worshiped...

...I broke.

WAR AND LOVE

Weeks passed after Abram and Lot's separation—weeks in which my body learned what my soul still could not accept.

I learned to cook their meals. I learned to grind grain with their stones. I learned to milk the goats and drink their milk. I learned to churn butter with my rough hands. I learned to make unleavened bread. I learned to speak like them, move like them, not get in the way, not disturb.

Not because I wanted to... but because I could not afford to fail. I was already carrying enough pain; I could not bear more caused by negligence.

So I drew breath from where there was none. I forced myself to be useful. To be invisible. To be perfect. To be whatever was necessary so I would not become a problem.

And in the midst of that silent effort, one day I heard screams.

Shepherds running. Men panting. Faces full of anguish. Something terrible had happened.

My first thought was cattle—some beast, some attack, some loss.

But when the men reached Abram, I saw him fall to the ground. I saw his hands cover his head. I saw his body bend as if pain had pierced him.

I froze.

I had never seen a leader react like that. In Egypt, pharaohs did not lament. They commanded. They punished. They shouted. But they did not break.

Abram did.

And that confused me.

Was it because of the cattle? Did he love his animals so deeply? Was he so sensitive? Or had something worse happened?

I didn't understand… I only watched from afar, as always—discreet, silent, invisible.

Abram stepped aside. I saw him speaking to himself—or perhaps to that God who cannot be seen, that God without a statue, without a form, without a face, the God he worshiped with a devotion I could not comprehend.

When he finished, he gathered all his shepherds, all his servants, all the men.

It was like a great assembly. And there, at last, I understood what had happened.

Kings… Wars… Conflicts… Battles.

And in the midst of all that… Lot had been taken captive.

The nephew he loved. The young man who had chosen the valley. The man who had left with his family.

NO AROMA

Abram did not hesitate… He did not tremble… He did not complain.

He simply said he would go and rescue him.

And then I saw something that left me speechless.

Peasants. Shepherds. Men without swords. Without armor. Without shields. Without military training.

Only shepherds' staffs. Only calloused hands. Only willing hearts.

It was madness… Absolute madness.

I had seen Egypt's army—war chariots, spears, shields, endless rows of soldiers, discipline, strength, power.

And now I saw these men—simple men—preparing to face kings.

But what struck me most was not the madness… It was love.

Abram's love for Lot—a love so great it led him to risk everything. A love that asked for nothing in return. A love I had never seen. A love I had never received.

And as I watched that man—as I saw his determination, as I saw him move out of love—something inside me broke again.

I thought:

"If I had had someone like that in my life… I would have rescued myself long ago."

But I hadn't. I never had. I never had a love that fought for me. Never had an embrace that searched for me. Never had a name that defended me.

And as they prepared to leave, I sank deeper into my own abyss.

They went to rescue Lot.

And I stayed behind… hoping that someone, someday, might want to rescue me.

THE SOLITUDE OF THE CAMP AND THE RETURN

When the men left, the camp fell silent—a strange, hollow silence, as if even the wind had gone with them.

Only the women and children remained—the wives of shepherds, the mothers of young men, the sisters of the boys who had marched with Abram.

At first I expected fear. Tears. Desperation.

But no.

What I saw was something I had never witnessed in my life. The women gathered. They embraced one another. They encouraged one another. They shared bread, water, words. They sat together around the fire. They prayed. They spoke to that invisible God with a confidence that baffled me.

I watched them from a corner… Always from a corner… Always from afar.

I saw how they cared for one another—not only about food or clothing, but about what they felt, what they feared, what they hoped.

It was a warm love. An everyday love. A love that did not need temples or golden columns.

And then I remembered Egypt's palace—its coldness, its silent corridors, the women who served without speaking, the mothers who did not embrace, the men who never looked into each other's eyes.

And I felt an emptiness inside me.

I thought:

"How beautiful it would be if one day someone called me by my name… with love… with tenderness… and simply asked, 'How are you feeling today?'"

But no one did. No one ever had. No one had ever loved me like that. No one had ever understood me.

And to be honest… I began to believe I had not been born for that.

As nostalgia sank me, as my heart shrank, as my soul curled like a dry leaf…

…the men returned.

We heard them before we saw them—their voices, their laughter, their strong steps, their shouts of victory.

When they appeared, their faces were shining. There was something about them—a light, a strength, a joy that illuminated everything around them.

Lot had been rescued. All the goods recovered. They returned without wounds. Without blood. Without death.

I did not understand how it was possible—how shepherds could defeat kings, how men without swords could return victorious.

But the women asked no questions.

They ran.

They embraced their husbands, their children, their fathers, their brothers.

It was a festival of love—an outburst of joy, a river of hugs and tears and laughter.

And for a moment—just a moment—I felt their joy as if it were mine.

Though none of those men loved me, though none of those arms were for me, though my heart was splintered and ready to break into a thousand pieces… a smile appeared on my face.

That night there was a great banquet—food, music, laughter, stories of the battle, prayers of gratitude.

And I slept under the stars, looking at the sky, thinking:

"Maybe that invisible God… maybe He really does help them."

And with that thought…

…I fell asleep.

THE TIME OF PEACE

As the days passed after the victory and the men's return, the camp slowly settled back into its ordinary rhythm—the noise of animals, the smell of freshly baked bread, the sound of women grinding grain, the laughter of children running between the tents.

And I… I adapted.

As I always had.

NO AROMA

I adapted to my father's absence. I adapted to my mother's absence. I adapted to the palace in Egypt. I adapted to slavery. I adapted to silence. I adapted to pain.

And now I was adapting to this new life— to these people, to their customs, to their food, to their language, to their invisible God.

I no longer cried at night. I no longer asked why. I no longer expected anything. I simply lived. I simply breathed. I simply did what I had to do.

And in that strange calm, one night, I heard something.

It wasn't a scream. It wasn't a song. It wasn't the women praying.

It was Abram's voice.

He stepped out of his tent with his face lit by something I could not understand. He walked to a secluded place, as he always did when he wanted to speak with his God.

I followed him with my eyes, never approaching. I never approached. It was not my place.

I saw him lift his face to the heavens. I saw him speak. I saw him listen. I saw him respond.

It was a conversation—a real conversation—with someone I could not see. And then I heard words that were not meant for me, yet still passed through me like an arrow.

Abram spoke of fear. Of the future. Of inheritance. Of children he did not have. Of promises I did not understand.

And then… silence.

A silence so deep it felt as if the entire sky were listening.

Abram looked up. He looked at the stars. And his face changed—as if he had received an answer, as if he had seen something I could not see.

I did not hear the voice… I did not hear the words… I did not hear the promise.

But I saw the effect.

I saw his body relax. I saw his breathing slow. I saw his eyes shine with a hope I had never known.

And I thought:

"How easy it is for some to believe. How easy it is for some to wait. How easy it is for some to receive words of love."

I had no promises. I had no inheritance. I had no future. I had no voice speaking to me from heaven.

But I was alive… I was breathing… I was learning… I was surviving.

And for me, that was enough.

Abram returned to his tent with a peace I had never seen in a man—a peace that came from a God I did not understand, a God who spoke, a God who promised, a God who saw.

I remained outside, looking at the stars—thinking of nothing, thinking of everything, thinking of how life had taught me to forget my wounds just enough to keep walking.

And that night, for the first time in a long time, it did not hurt to remember. It did not hurt to exist. It did not hurt to be alone.

I simply breathed…

…And I fell asleep.

Chapter 6

"THE BREAK"

The Tear That Made Me Bleed and Suffer

It was a clear morning. The wind gently shook the tents. The goats bleated. Children ran through the ashes of last night's fires. The women laughed as they prepared the bread.

Everything was normal. Everything was as usual. And I… I was also as always—doing my tasks, breathing, living, adapting.

But something changed.

I saw Abram and Sarai standing apart. It wasn't unusual for them to speak, but this time… this time something was different.

Sarai was gesturing sharply. Her hands moved as if demanding something. Her face was tense, rigid, clinging to a truth I could not hear.

Abram, on the other hand, wore the expression I had only seen in men who no longer have options—like someone carrying a weight he never asked for, listening to something he did not want to accept.

I watched from afar. Not out of curiosity… but because after nine years living with them, I knew their gestures, their silences, their looks.

And this… this was different.

As I wondered, they stopped speaking. And then it happened.

They both turned their heads toward me.

THE BREAK

They looked at me. Both of them. At the same time.

That look changed everything.

A chill ran down my spine. My heart began to race. My hands trembled.

The subject was me.

I was the conversation. I was the problem. I was the decision.

Questions flooded me— fast, desperate, suffocating.

Did I do something wrong? Did I fail at a task? Did I offend someone? Did I neglect something? Did I say something I shouldn't have?

The intrigue grew. Anxiety tightened my chest. I felt something dark approaching.

Because that was my life: every time I adapted, every time I accepted, every time I managed to breathe without pain… something came to strike me inside and remind me that my wounds were not healed—only forgotten.

And then I saw them walking toward me.

Abram… Sarai… Together. With firm steps. With a purpose I did not understand.

My body began to tremble. My breath shortened. My mind filled with fear.

What did I do? What is going to happen to me? Why are they coming to me?

When they reached me, there was no introduction. No gentleness. No explanation.

Only an order… An order that froze my soul.

THE BREAK

Sarai, with a hard voice, without emotion, without looking me in the eyes, said:

"You will sleep with Abram. You will conceive a son for me."

I did not understand… I did not react… I did not breathe.

I was paralyzed— as if my body no longer belonged to me, as if my soul had stepped aside so it would not feel.

There were no questions. No compassion. No humanity.

Only an order—cold, cruel, bare.

The wind seemed to stop, as if even the air refused to touch me after hearing those words. And in that moment, I understood something that pierced me like a blade:

I was not a woman… I was an object. A vessel. A tool. A body others could use.

The vilest thing that had ever happened to me. The most humiliating. The most painful.

I wanted to speak… I wanted to ask why… I wanted to say something—anything.

But I couldn't.

My voice would not come. My mind would not think. My heart would not beat.

I only wished I could return to the night before, when I looked at the stars and for a moment believed I was fine.

But I was no longer fine… I was no longer free… I was no longer myself.

I was… whatever they decided I was.

THE NIGHT MY SOUL HID

When Abram entered my tent, the air changed. The smell of dust and wool mixed with a silence so dense it seemed to carry weight of its own.

It wasn't a sound. It wasn't a wind. It was something deeper—like when a shadow falls over a field and the light doesn't know where to hide.

I didn't look at him. I couldn't. My body was there, but my soul had already begun to walk away.

It was an ancient mechanism—one I had learned without being taught: when life hurt me, I left. I escaped inward. I hid in a secret corner where no one could reach me.

As he approached, I closed my eyes and let my mind build a different world. A world where I was not an object. A world where my name carried weight. A world where someone asked me how I felt.

In my imagination, I stood in a field of lilies. The lilies moved as if they knew my name—as if they recognized me more than any human ever had.

The wind moved the flowers like a white sea. The mountains were gentle. The sky was whole.

And I walked barefoot—without fear, without orders, without chains.

In that invented place, I was free.

Meanwhile, in the tent, my body remained still, obedient, silent.

I heard no words. No tenderness. No name spoken.

Only the sound of my own breathing, trying not to break.

In my fantasy, a great tree gave me shade. Its branches were strong. Its leaves were many. And I leaned against its trunk as if seeking refuge.

That tree was my escape. My hiding place. My imagined protection.

Because in reality… there was none.

No shelter…

…No shade…

…No embrace.

Only an act I did not choose, a destiny I did not ask for, a wound opening without a sound.

My mind clung to the fantasy like a castaway clings to a piece of wood—and beneath it all, the imagined sound of distant waters.

Time passed… I don't know how much. I don't know how. I don't know in what order.

I only know that in my invented world, the wind kept moving the lilies, and I kept walking far, far away—as far as I could go without disappearing.

Until I heard a sound.

A step. A movement. Fabric shifting.

I opened my eyes…

…Abram was leaving the tent.

He said nothing. He did not look back. He did not seek my eyes. He did not say my name.

He simply left.

And when the curtain fell again, the fantasy dissolved like smoke.

I was alone. In silence. With my body still and my soul in pieces.

And I thought:

“I wish I could stay forever in the field of lilies.”

THE DAY MY BODY SPOKE BEFORE MY MIND

When I woke, the tent was quiet—a heavy, thick quiet, as if the air itself knew what had happened.

I sat up slowly. My body felt strange, unfamiliar, as if it no longer belonged to me. There was a discomfort I could not name—a mixture of shame, pain, and something deeper… something I did not want to face.

I felt the urge to wash myself—to rinse away the night before, to erase what had happened, to tear off the feeling of being used.

But as I washed, I discovered something that stopped me.

It wasn’t pain. It wasn’t dirt. It wasn’t only the memory.

It was… a change. A faint warmth rising from my belly, like an ember hidden beneath the sand.

A silent change. An inward change. A change that did not come from outside, but from within.

I knew my body. I had observed it all my life—how it responded to tiredness, how it tightened in fear, how it softened in rare moments of peace.

But this… this was different.

It was as if a spark had ignited in a place I had never felt before—a faint sensation, almost imperceptible, but real.

I stood still. Very still. Listening to my own body like someone listening for a whisper behind a door.

And then I understood.

Not with words… Not with logic… Not with certainty.

I understood with the ancient instinct of women—a knowledge not learned, but revealed.

Something had begun inside me. Something small. Something fragile. Something I had not asked for. Something I had not chosen. Something I did not know if I wanted.

But something… alive.

I sat on the floor of the tent and placed my hand on my belly—not out of tenderness, but out of bewilderment.

It was as if my body spoke before my mind, as if it whispered:

"Something is growing here."

And I did not know whether to cry, to tremble, to run, or simply accept that my life had just changed forever.

The unpleasant feeling remained—a shadow behind me—but behind that shadow, far behind, there was a tiny light, a spark, a beginning.

Conception. Mystery. The start of something that did not yet have a name.

And as the camp woke outside, I sat in silence, trying to understand how something born of pain could also feel... formidable.

TWO MONTHS OF SILENCE AND STARES THAT AVOID

The days that followed were strange—not because of what I did, but because of what I stopped seeing.

My routine did not change. I woke early. I ground the grain. I tended the goats. I carried water. I helped the women. I did everything I had always done.

But something in the air had shifted—as if the camp breathed differently.

Abram, who had always been distant, became even more distant—not with indifference, but with avoidance.

One morning, we crossed paths between the tents. He was walking toward me. I lowered my gaze, as always. But before we met, he changed direction.

The dust rose between us like a small wall— enough to remind me that something had broken.

He turned his body. He averted his eyes. As if my presence were a shadow he did not want to pass through.

It wasn't contempt. It was fear—a fear that wasn't his, but borrowed. A fear with Sarai's name.

Because Sarai... she had changed too.

THE BREAK

She used to send me to Abram—with water, with bread, with cloth, with messages. But now she sent another servant. Anyone but me.

It was as if I had been marked—not with ink, not with words, but with a silence that said:

"Do not come near."

And I understood—not because they explained it, but because I saw it in their eyes.

Sarai watched me... Not always… Not directly… But I felt it. Like someone observing an experiment, waiting for a result. Like someone watching a vessel to see if it cracks. Like someone guarding a seed to see if it sprouts.

When I lifted my head, she looked away—quickly, as if she didn't want me to know she had been watching.

But even in that quick movement, there was a flash I could not decipher—fear, pain, or perhaps a reflection of my own wound.

And so the days passed… And the weeks… And the months.

My routine stayed the same. But the atmosphere… the atmosphere was different.

Abram avoiding me. Sarai watching me. Women whispering. Men silent. The camp breathing differently.

And I… I had changed too.

Not on the outside… Inside.

There was something in my body—something small, something silent, something growing without asking permission.

I knew my rhythms.

I knew my signs.

I knew my cycles.

I knew my fatigue.

And this… this was not fatigue. Not hunger. Not stress. Not sadness.

It was something else. Something new. Something undeniable.

After two months, it was no longer intuition. No longer suspicion. No longer imagination.

It was certainty.

I was pregnant.

And while the camp continued its life, I walked with a hand on my belly—not out of tenderness, but out of disbelief.

Because inside me, in silence, without anyone knowing, without anyone celebrating, without anyone wanting it… something was growing…

…Something that would change everything.

THE PRIDE THAT SPRANG FROM MY WOUND

As the days went by, something shifted inside me. Not only in my body—in my mind, in my way of seeing the world.

It was as if, after a lifetime of feeling "less," I had suddenly found a place where I was "more."

It wasn't true. It wasn't healthy. It wasn't fair. But it was what my wounded mind needed to believe.

Because while Sarai suffered for what she could not have, I carried something inside me that she had never achieved—something she longed for, something life had denied her.

And that idea… that idea poisoned me.

Not with malice—but with pain.

With the ache of so many years of being nothing, that when I finally had "something," I clung to it as if it were my identity.

Abram avoided me… Sarai watched me… The camp murmured.

And I… I walked with my hand on my belly—not out of tenderness, but out of pride.

A clumsy pride. A wounded pride. Born not from strength, but from a fracture. It was like a bitter taste in the mouth—it did not nourish, but it deceived the hunger.

When Sarai watched me from afar, I would lower my gaze to my belly, run my hand over it, and then lift my eyes to her with a small smile—a quiet message wrapped in silence.

A message I never spoke aloud, but repeated inside me like an echo:

"I am your slave… but I carry within me what you cannot have."

It was cruel… It was unfair… It was arrogant.

But it was my way of surviving—my way of believing I had value, my way of escaping the feeling of being nothing.

Sarai sensed it.

She felt it.

She breathed it.

And her gaze hardened each day—not with hatred, but with pain, with fear, with insecurity.

I did not understand then.

I did not see her wound… I only saw mine.

And so two months passed—two months in which my belly was still small, but my pride grew like a shadow.

Two months in which I was still a slave, but inside me something was growing that would change everything.

Two months in which the atmosphere tightened, like a rope stretched to its limit.

Until I could no longer deny it:

I was pregnant.

And that pregnancy—which could have been a miracle—became the beginning of a silent war between two broken women.

WHEN MY PRIDE BECAME A WEAPON AGAINST ME

As the days passed, my belly remained small—but my attitude… my attitude grew like a shadow I did not know how to control.

It wasn't strength… It wasn't confidence… It wasn't victory.

It was pain in disguise. Trauma dressed as triumph. An illusion I built so I wouldn't feel so small.

Because my whole life had been "less"—less seen, less loved, less important, less human.

And now, for the first time, there was something inside me that was not "less." Something Sarai wanted. Something she did not have. Something life had withheld from her.

And that idea… that idea transformed me.

When Sarai watched me from afar, I would lower my gaze to my belly, run my hand gently over it, and then lift my eyes to her with a smile that was neither kind nor humble nor innocent.

It was a small smile, but charged with a silent message—a message I never spoke aloud, but repeated within me like a poisonous whisper:

"You are the wife… but I carry within me what you have not been able to have."

It wasn't malice… It was woundedness—the voice of a girl who had never been loved and now believed she had found a place to feel valuable.

But that illusion did not lift me… It drowned me.

Because while I felt "superior," I was still a slave. Still nameless. Still without rights. Still without a voice.

And Sarai… Sarai saw everything.

She saw my gaze.

She saw my gesture.

She saw my pride.

She saw my fantasy.

And every time I lifted my head, she lowered hers—not out of shame, but out of pain.

A pain I did not understand then. A pain I ignored because I was too busy trying to feel like "something."

The atmosphere grew tense—heavier, more fragile.

The women noticed. The men sensed it. The entire camp seemed to hold its breath.

And so the days passed… And the weeks… And the months.

Until there was no doubt:

I was pregnant.

And that pregnancy—which could have been a bridge—became a wall.

A wall between Sarai and me.

A wall between Abram and me.

A wall between my past and my future.

A wall I myself had begun to build—with every look, every gesture, every proud thought born from my wound.

And as that wall grew, my name returned to haunt me:

Hagar — the fugitive…

…Always running, even when it looked like I was moving forward.

Chapter 7

"THE ESCAPE"

I don't know the exact moment it began. There was no first scream. No warning. Just a shift in the air—a change you feel before you hear.

Sarai had been watching me for days. Days swallowing words. Days carrying a pain that had nowhere to go.

And I… without realizing it, fed that pain. With my looks. With my pride. With that small smile I mistook for victory—a smile that, for her, was a dagger.

Until one day, the rope snapped.

Sarai erupted—not because she hated me, but because she could no longer contain the weight of her own wound.

I heard it before I saw it. Her voice tore through the camp like thunder.

"Abram! This is your fault!"

I froze. The women stopped grinding. The children stopped running. The shepherds stopped speaking.

The entire camp turned to stone.

Sarai stepped out of her tent, her eyes blazing—not with hatred, but with pain so deep it had turned into fury.

"My wrong be upon you!" she cried to Abram.

THE ESCAPE

"I put my servant into your arms, and now that she has conceived, she looks down on me!"

The ground opened beneath my feet. Not because she lied—but because she spoke the truth.

My pride had wounded her… My gaze had humiliated her… My fantasy had pierced her.

But I said nothing. I couldn't. I shouldn't. It was not my place.

Abram stood between us—caught between two pains, unable to heal either.

He listened in silence. He did not raise his voice. He did not contradict her. He did not defend me.

He simply looked at her with the expression I already knew—the expression of a man carrying a burden he never asked for.

Sarai's voice cracked between rage and tears.

"May the Lord judge between you and me!"

Abram inhaled deeply—the breath of someone who has run out of answers.

And then he spoke the words that changed my life:

"Your servant is in your hands. Do with her whatever seems good to you."

A coldness rose from my feet—as if the earth itself withdrew its warmth from me.

He did not say it cruelly. He did not say it with contempt. He said it with resignation—with the helplessness of a man who no longer knew what to do.

But for me…

…those words were a sentence.

And immediately, the mistreatment began.

Sarai turned toward me—not with hatred, but with an open wound searching for a place to bleed.

And I was the place.

She did not strike me… She did not shout at me… She did not insult me.

It was worse.

She ignored me. She diminished me. She treated me as if I did not exist—as if I were air, as if I were an object that cluttered her path.

She gave me orders without looking at me. Sent me to do impossible tasks. Made me repeat work I had already done. Corrected me for things that were not wrong. Made me feel as if every breath was a mistake.

Sometimes, when she passed by, her shadow brushed against me—and that slight touch hurt more than any blow.

And I… I allowed it.

Because I was still a slave.

Still voiceless.

Still nameless… Still without the right to defend myself.

And because, deep down, I knew my pride had ignited this storm.

As Sarai poured her pain onto me, my body changed. My belly grew. My breathing grew heavier. My back ached. My strength faded.

But I could not stop… I could not rest… I could not ask for help.

Each day was harder. Each day more painful. Each day more evident that I could not continue like this.

But I still did not flee. I was not running yet. I had not escaped.

Because I still believed I could endure it. Because I still thought pain was part of my destiny. Because I still did not know that God was watching me.

WHEN I COULD NO LONGER INVENT ANOTHER WORLD

At first, I tried to do what I had always done. Close my eyes. Invent a landscape. Build a world where I could hide—a field of lilies, a great tree, a sky without cracks.

But this time… it didn't work.

It was as if the doors of my mind had been sealed from within, leaving me trapped with my own pain.

Every time Sarai humiliated me, every time she gave me an impossible task, every time she treated me as if I were nothing—I tried to escape inward.

But there was nowhere to go.

My mind, which had always been my refuge, became a dark room with no windows—a place where the walls closed in, a place with no lilies, no wind, no shade.

For the first time in my life, I had to feel everything.

The pain… The humiliation… The loneliness… The sense of being less than nothing… The certainty that my life was not going to change… The belief that my destiny was to suffer and that there was no way out.

And that… that broke me…

Once again…

…I broke.

THE COLLAPSE

One afternoon, while doing a task Sarai had made me repeat three times, something inside me broke.

It wasn't a scream. It wasn't a blow. It wasn't a word.

It was a thought.

A thought that fell on me like a stone:

"This is never going to change."

And when that thought entered, everything else collapsed.

My hands trembled. My legs weakened. A buzzing filled my ears, as if the world were shutting down around me. My breathing turned into a cry— a cry I could not stop, a cry born from years of wounds, from absences, from silences, from nights without a name.

I cried like a child—like the baby who once had a father who protected her and a mother who loved her. I cried for that lost girl. I cried for myself. I cried for who I was. I cried for who I would never be.

THE ESCAPE

And in that crying, in that collapse, in that mixture of anguish and despair, something inside me screamed:

"I can't take this anymore!"

I didn't think… I didn't plan… I didn't evaluate.

I simply stood up.

My hands pulled back the curtain of the tent. My eyes, full of tears, searched the horizon. My body moved before my mind.

And I ran.

I ran as if my name pushed me from behind: Hagar — the fugitive.

I ran like someone escaping fire. Like someone fleeing death. Like someone searching for air after being underwater too long.

I ran without looking back. Without thinking of Abram. Without thinking of Sarai. Without thinking of the camp. Without thinking of anything.

I ran as if every step were an opportunity, as if each stride were hope, as if the desert could give me what life had denied me.

I ran because the alternative was to die inside.

I ran because I could no longer invent another world.

I ran because I needed a real one.

And for the first time in my life, I was doing something different:

I was running.

Running toward the desert. Toward the unknown. Toward the only place where I could still breathe.

THE ESCAPE

RUNNING FOR THE SOUL TO REACH THE BODY

I ran.

At first, my legs moved instinctively—as if my body knew before my mind that staying meant dying inside.

But soon, something else ran with me.

My heart.

It beat hard—so hard it felt as if it wanted to break through my chest and flee as well.

And as I ran, my mind ignited like a bonfire fed by years of pain.

Each step was a memory. Each stride a wound. Each breath a fragment of my story.

I saw my father… I saw my mother… I saw the palace… I saw the hands that handed me over… I saw the nights of loneliness… I saw the humiliations… I saw the looks… I saw the orders… I saw the tent… I saw the mistreatment… I saw my pride… I saw my fall.

Everything flashed quickly—like a film someone rewinds without mercy.

And that pain, instead of stopping me, propelled me.

It was fuel. It was fire. It was fear. It was rage. It was life.

The sun beat down on my skin without mercy.

Hot air entered my lungs like embers, burning every attempt to breathe. The air was dry, harsh, as if it wanted to steal my breath.

The sand burned my feet. The wind pushed against me. The heat wrapped me like a blanket of fire.

But none of that stopped me.

Because for the first time in my life, I wasn't running from someone—I was running toward something.

Toward a place where I could breathe…

…Toward a place where I could exist…

…Toward a place where my soul was not a burden.

But the body… the body has limits.

My legs shook. My breathing became a groan. My throat burned. My vision blurred. My belly felt heavy. My back ached.

It was too much—too much for a pregnant woman, too much for a tired slave, too much for a broken heart.

But my thoughts were racing, desperate, full of anguish—and I could not stop.

And then I saw it.

A flash… A glimmer… A small, distant, but unmistakably real light.

I didn't know what it was—water, metal, or a heat-born illusion.

But I saw it. And I believed.

It was a small glimmer, but in my state it looked like a beacon—as if the desert itself were guiding me toward judgment or salvation.

I thought it was a sign… I thought it was a calling… I thought it was a place where I could fall without shattering.

And with the last strength I had, with a burst I didn't know was in me, I ran toward that light.

I ran as if my life depended on reaching it. I ran as if my soul were ahead, waiting for me. I ran as if the desert were a bridge and not a tomb.

When I arrived, my knees gave out. My hands touched the ground. My chest searched for air like someone searching for life.

And there it was.

A spring. A well. Water—the very thing I needed.

Water in the desert… Water in my despair… Water in my collapse.

I fell beside the spring—trembling, crying, breathing as if I had just been born.

And so my escape ended: Me… by the water… broken… emptied… but alive.

THE VICTORY THAT TASTED OF WATER AND DECEPTION

When I reached the well, I didn't think. I didn't reason. I didn't pray. I simply threw myself into the water.

My trembling hands plunged into it as if touching a miracle. I brought it to my mouth in desperation—drinking like an animal that has run too far, like a runaway camel that finally finds an oasis.

The water tasted metallic, ancient—as if it had waited centuries to touch my lips.

It slid down my throat like extinguished fire.

I felt my body absorb it greedily, each sip giving me back a little life, each handful cooling my burning skin as I poured it over my face.

And then… I laughed.

First a small, incredulous laugh—as if I didn't understand what was happening.

Then a laugh—a full, free, overflowing laugh, as if I were celebrating an immense victory.

Because in that instant, in that first minute by the water, I felt something I had never felt:

victory.

Not a real victory… Not a deep victory… Not a victory that heals.

A prisoner's victory.

A fugitive's victory.

A victory that tasted like freedom… and also like guilt.

An illegal victory.

A stolen victory.

But a victory nonetheless.

I laughed like someone breaking a silence of years. Like someone doing something for herself for the first time. Like someone daring to defy a destiny that seemed carved in stone.

It was a superficial joy—but it was mine. A spark of happiness stolen from pain. A moment where I felt free, even if only on the outside.

THE ESCAPE

As the water ran down my face, my breathing began to calm. The trembling in my hands eased. My heart stopped beating like a war drum. My exhausted body began to slow down.

And there, in that descent, in that return to a normal rhythm, I began to hear myself.

Not my laughter. Not my breathing. Not the water.

But my truth.

It was the conscience that comes after relief—like the thief who escapes prison and suddenly realizes he is now "free"… but illegally free.

That was me.

I had escaped… I had run… I had broken my silence with actions… I had done the unthinkable.

But nothing inside me had healed. Nothing inside me had changed. Nothing inside me had been resolved.

Only the scenery had changed—not the wound. It was as if I had fled one cage only to enter another—larger, quieter, more mine.

And that awareness fell on me like a long shadow.

Because I was no longer inventing worlds inside my mind. Now I was inventing worlds with my actions—and that was far more dangerous.

It was as if my fantasies had left my head and turned into real decisions, real paths, real escapes.

And for the first time, I asked myself:

How far can my thoughts take me when I don't know how to handle my pain?

I stood still—very still—water dripping from my face, the desert breathing around me, my belly pulsing softly beneath my hand.

And I understood something that frightened me:

I was not free… I was only far away.

And that difference…

…that difference was an abyss.

Chapter 8

"THE ENCOUNTER"

The Voice of the Messenger in the Wilderness

I lay beside the well, my cheek pressed against the damp sand, my face still wet, my heart finally quiet.

It wasn't peace. It was exhaustion—the silence that remains after too much crying.

My body was still, but my mind was open, like a sponge absorbing everything around it.

I felt the warm breeze. The sandy air. The thin shadow of a nearby bush. The sunlight filtering through my eyelashes.

It was as if all my senses had awakened at once.

And in that moment of stillness, I saw him.

A man on the horizon…

In the distance, between light and sand, a man was walking toward me.

He did not run…

…He did not hurry…

…He did not look lost.

He walked with a confidence I had never seen in any man.

He wore no armor, yet walked like a warrior.

He wore no crown, yet walked like a king.

He carried no insignias, yet walked like someone who needed no proof of who he was.

The closer he came, the more I tried to understand him. The air around him seemed to ripple, as if the desert heat recognized him and moved aside in his wake.

But the more I thought, the less sense it made.

So I told myself:

"I'm at a well… He must be coming for water."

And as always, I minimized it.

Because I had learned to believe that no one came for me. That no one looked for me. That no one saw me. That I had been born to be ignored.

So I lowered my gaze. I avoided his eyes. I hid from another possible wound.

I made myself small… Invisible… Silent.

And then the air conspired with him…

I heard it… The Voice.

The sound did not enter through my ears— it entered through my bones, as if my own body were the instrument chosen for that Voice to resonate.

It was not a human voice. Not an ordinary voice. Not a voice one forgets.

It thundered inside my chest as if I had been waiting my entire life to hear it.

THE ENCOUNTER

A voice with a strange frequency—as if it came from far away and from deep within at the same time.

A voice that made the air vibrate. A voice that stirred the water in the well. A voice with weight. With glory. With strength.

A voice like thunder, yet not frightening. Like fire, yet not burning. Like a mighty wind, yet not pushing.

A voice that, if a cedar had been near, would have shattered it. If a forest had been around, would have stripped it bare.

A voice that made the desert tremble.

And that Voice… that Voice spoke my name…

…AGAR.

My name fell on me like cool water on a burning stone, breaking something inside me that had been hardened for years.

Not “servant.” … Not “slave.” … Not “Egyptian.” … Not “she.”

My name.

My real name. My full name. My name that almost no one used.

And then, in a language I did not know yet understood as if it had always been mine, He said:

“AGAR, SERVANT OF SARAI, WHERE DO YOU COME FROM AND WHERE ARE YOU GOING?”

And when I heard that question, the world stopped.

The water stilled… The wind paused… The sun held its breath. Even my shadow froze, as if it too were listening.

Everything remained still.

Except my heart… My heart opened.

And for one second—a second that felt like an entire day—I stood before a Voice that called me by name in the middle of the desert.

THE NAME THAT GAVE ME BACK MY SOUL

When that Voice spoke my name, something inside me stopped.

Not my legs. Not my breath. Not my body.

My soul.

It was as if a door that had been locked for years burst open.

AGAR.

My name. My real name. My full name. My name that had been forgotten, buried, silenced.

And the instant I heard it, my mind ran faster than when I fled the camp.

In fractions of a second, I thought:

How does he know my name?

If he knows my name… does he know my story?

My life?

My parents?

My pain?

Because calling me by my name was not just knowledge—it was intention.

Intention to come close. Intention to see me. Intention to recognize me. Intention to treat me as a person. As a woman. As a human being.

With a single word, that Man gave me back something I had lost long ago:

…my human identity.

And while I tried to understand, He spoke again.

"Servant of Sarai."

Those words pierced me like an arrow. Not insult. Not contempt. Not humiliation.

Truth.

A truth that hurt, but also anchored me—as if that phrase were the rope keeping my soul from dissolving in the wind.

A truth I had tried to escape.

A truth I had wanted to forget.

A truth I had buried under fantasies, illusions, pride, flight.

"Servant of Sarai."

First He gave me my name…

Then He gave me my reality…

It was as if He were saying:

"I know who you are. I know who you were. I know where you come from. I know what you're running from."

And that combination—name and truth—cornered me.

He did not let me invent stories. He did not let me escape inward. He did not let me hide in fantasies.

He left me naked before myself…

Time stood still…

Being in His presence was like being in another dimension.

Time did not move forward, but it did not stop either. Everything was suspended— as if the entire desert held its breath.

I did not know who He was. But I knew He was not an ordinary man.

There was something in His presence. Something in His voice. Something in His eyes.

Something not of this world.

And then came the question that opened my past and my future:

"Where do you come from and where are you going?"

At first, I didn't understand. If He knew I was Sarai's servant, then He knew where I came from. He knew what I was fleeing. He knew what had happened.

Why ask?

But then I understood.

He wasn't asking about the path. He was asking about my roots. My story. My identity. My destiny. My purpose.

It was as if He were saying:

"Who are you really? And where do you think you're going?"

And that question unearthed a memory I had kept like a broken treasure.

It entered me like a thin beam of light, searching for cracks to illuminate what I had tried to hide.

The memory of my father. The memory of my mother. The memory of that messenger of God who, according to my mother, told my father that I would be great—a great woman.

Maybe this Man wanted me to remember. Maybe not.

But I remembered.

And that memory—along with my name, along with the truth, along with the question—opened a space inside my soul that I thought was dead. And when He asked me, it felt like a calling.

THE TRUTH IN MY MOUTH AND HEAVEN SPEAKING

After hearing my name in that Voice—after feeling my identity return to me like a river finding its course—I had no choice but to tell the truth.

I took a deep breath. A deep, trembling breath, like someone preparing to open a wound hidden for years.

And I said:

"I am fleeing from my mistress."

I didn't say it with pride. I didn't say it in rebellion. I didn't say it in shame.

I said it truthfully.

The truth came out of my mouth like a thin stream of water finally finding its path.

Because that Man—that Being—had awakened in me something I had not felt since childhood:

trust.

I could not lie to Him. I could not deceive Him. I did not want to hide anything from Him.

There was something in Him that reminded me of my father—those memories I keep like broken treasures: a mixture of trembling, peace, vulnerability, and safety.

It was as if I knew He would not hurt me. As if I knew He loved me without knowing me. As if I knew He had come for me.

And just when I thought I had said the hardest thing, He spoke again:

"Return to your mistress and submit yourself under her hand."

My heart cried inside:

What?

But my thoughts were stronger than my emotions. Because that Man—that Messenger—could not give me harmful counsel. He could not send me into destruction. He could not be wrong.

His authority was not human. His wisdom was not earthly. His presence was not of this world.

And before I could process His command, He continued.

He gave me a prophecy—a word from the future:

“I will multiply your descendants exceedingly, so that they shall not be numbered for multitude.”

The air vibrated around us, as if the desert recognized words spoken before to other chosen men.

My mind searched desperately for where I had heard those words.

And then I remembered.

In Abram’s camp—the stories they told about their God, the God who called him from distant lands, the God who promised him countless descendants.

And I thought:

“The God of Abram… He is speaking to me.”

To me. To the slave. To the foreigner. To the broken woman. To the one who fled. To the one no one saw.

Me.

And He continued:

“Behold, you are with child.”

My heart stopped.

How did He know? How could He see what was not yet visible? How could He know what was hidden inside me?

And then:

“You shall bear a son, and you shall call his name Ishmael, for the LORD has heard your affliction.”

THE ENCOUNTER

When I heard that Name—that Name I cannot repeat,that Name I cannot pronounce, that Name only He can say—it was as if the sky leaned toward me, as if the sand beneath my knees softened, as if the entire universe whispered my name at once and my body could not bear it.

I fell.

I fell to my knees. I fell with my hands on the sand. I fell with my forehead against the burning ground. I fell into worship.

Not because I was weak. But because my soul recognized its Master before my mind understood Him.

Not because He commanded it. Not because I was intimidated. Not because I was afraid.

I fell because my soul recognized its Creator.

Not the messenger. Not the man. Not the figure.

But the God who sent Him.

That message made me greater than a king…

And when He said:

"YHWH has heard your affliction,"

something inside me broke, and something inside me was rebuilt at the same time.

Because He didn't just know me…

…He didn't just know my name

…He didn't just know my story

…He didn't just know my pain.

He had heard me.

Me—the slave, the invisible one, the one no one defended, the one no one named, the one no one loved.

And He didn't just hear me—He sent me a Messenger. A special Messenger. A Messenger with words for the future. Words of purpose. Words spoken only to kings.

And in that moment, I felt greater than a king.

I felt loved…

…I felt seen.

…I felt cared for.

…I felt understood.

And with my forehead still on the sand, with my heart pounding, with my soul open wider than ever before,

I said:

"You are the God who sees me. The God who understands me. The God who knows me. The God who loves me."

And I named the well— the place where my life changed:

THE WELL OF THE LIVING ONE WHO SEES ME. THE WELL OF THE LIVING ONE WHO UNDERSTANDS ME. THE WELL OF THE LIVING ONE WHO LOVES ME.

A soft wind blew at that moment, as if the desert itself confirmed the name.

And on that day: a slave became a woman, a woman became a soul, and a soul was seen by the Living God.

THE RETURN

I returned to the camp at dawn on the third day. I don't know if anyone saw me first, or if it was the silence of the desert that announced my arrival, but as I walked between the first tents, I felt every eye turn toward me.

They were not looks of judgment. Nor mockery. It was as if they saw a familiar shadow carrying a new light they could not explain.

They looked surprised. Confused. Searching for a word they did not have.

Because I had left broken, empty, desperate—and I returned full.

Full of a Voice still burning in my chest. Full of a promise steadying my steps. Full of a name restored to me. Full of a love that came from no man.

Abram was the first to see me.

He stood at the entrance of his tent, speaking with a servant. When he saw me, his face changed.

Not joy.

Not anger.

A sigh.

A long, deep sigh—like someone seeing something he thought lost forever return.

Sarai stood behind him. She did not call me. She did not approach. She did not say my name. But she also sighed.

And in that sigh, I heard something I had never heard from her: recognition.

Not of my worth…

…Not of my pain…

…Not of my story.

But of her part in my flight.

I walked toward her without hesitation—not because I felt less, but because I no longer needed to prove anything.

I bowed—not as a slave, but as someone who knows her value no longer depends on anyone's gaze.

Not as the defeated, but as one who chooses peace.

"Forgive my attitude," I said.

"I am at your service."

She did not answer. She did not know how. She had no words for a woman who had returned different.

And I did not intend to explain it.

What I lived in the desert was not for them. Not to be told, analyzed, or discussed.

It was a treasure. My treasure.

A secret between Him and me. A well no one else would trample.

I returned to my duties—grinding grain, fetching water, caring for the animals, serving the table.

But every movement carried the echo of that Voice. Every step repeated the image of the Messenger. Every breath reminded me of where I had been found.

And so the months passed.

My belly grew. My hope grew with it.

Not a silent growth—a luminous one, as if each day not only a child but a promise was forming inside me.

I knew who I was.

I knew where I came from.

I knew where I was going.

And though no one else knew it, I walked through the camp as a woman who had been seen.

Chapter 9

"CHILDBIRTH"

The Intense Dance of Pain and Joy

The day of the birth came without warning. No signs. No dreams. No omens.

Just another sunrise—and a pain that began like a thin thread and grew into a wave that crossed me entirely.

The air inside the tent smelled of hot earth and sweat, as if the desert itself were breathing with me.

The women of the camp rushed in. They didn't speak to me, but they surrounded me with that mixture of urgency and ancient wisdom that only women carry when a life is about to break through.

Sarai was there. She didn't touch anything. She didn't help. She didn't give orders. She just watched.

Her fingers pressed against each other so tightly that her knuckles looked ready to tear through her skin.

And in her eyes, two fires burned at the same time: the fire of victory—for at last, through me, her barrenness would find a moment of relief—and the fire of defeat—because she knew, even if she never said it, that this son would not be hers.

Not completely.

Not deeply.

Not in what truly matters.

CHILDBIRTH

Each contraction felt like a tear—as if my body were opening from the inside to release something greater than the pain. But along with the pain, there was something else:

A primitive joy.

A strength that did not come from me.

A certainty that held me upright.

For every time the pain bent me, I heard the echo of that Voice in the wilderness: “I will multiply your descendants.” “You will bear a son.” “You will call him Ishmael.”

And that echo made me breathe.

The women held my arms. They gave me water. They whispered to me. But I could barely hear them.

My world had shrunk to a small circle: my body, my son, my promise.

Sarai stood motionless, like a statue cracked from within. Her eyes followed every movement, every gesture, every sound.

It wasn’t cruelty. It was hunger— a hunger for something life had denied her.

When the final moment came, I felt my body split in two. A scream escaped me—not from fear, but from strength. From life. From birth.

And then I heard it.

A cry… Small… Strong… New.

That sound went through me like a light breaking the night.

The women lifted him. Cleaned him. Wrapped him.

And placed him in my arms.

My son… My son… My son.

There was no greater word. No deeper truth. No brighter identity.

I looked at him. His eyes were closed, but his face was a promise— a seed, a beginning.

Sarai took one step forward. Only one. Then stopped.

On her face I saw something I had never seen before: pain and relief at the same time—as if this child were her victory and her deepest wound.

Abram arrived shortly after. He entered the tent slowly, as if afraid to interrupt something sacred.

The smell of the outside—dust, smoke, wool—came in with him, mixing with the warm scent of my newborn son.

When he saw the boy, his eyes lit up. Not with surprise. Not with doubt.

With pride.

A son.

A male.

An heir.

But when he looked at me, his expression changed. It wasn't love. It wasn't tenderness. It was something quieter. More complex.

Respect.

For I had given birth not only to a son—but to a promise.

And though no one knew it, though no one understood it, though no one even suspected it, I knew this child was not the fruit of pain, but of the Encounter.

The Encounter in the desert. The Encounter I kept as my treasure. The Encounter that gave me back my name.

I named him Ishmael.

As I spoke that name, the air inside the tent grew lighter—as if the sky itself nodded.

Because that is what He told me. Because that is how it had to be. Because that name was the mark of my story.

And as I held him, as his cry softened into breathing, as his small body settled on my chest, I knew that I had also been born that day.

MY SON, ISMAEL

Ishmael's early years were a gift no one else understood.

His laughter had a particular sound—like small bells struck by the wind.

As he grew, I learned to breathe again. Every time he opened his eyes, every sound he made, every small gesture, was a silent confirmation of what the Messenger had told me in the desert.

I carried a message from the future—and that message sustained me.

But in the camp, things were not so simple.

Sarai tried to convince herself that she was the mother of my child. She carried him more than necessary. She walked him between the tents as if he were a trophy—proof that her barrenness had been overcome.

She showed him to the women. Brought him near Abram. Held him with a strange mixture of pride and despair.

But when Ishmael was hungry, there was only one place where he found comfort. Only one body that could feed him. Only one breast that could give him life.

Mine.

And every time he clung to me, every time his crying died on my skin, every time his breathing slowed and deepened on my chest, I heard within me the words of the Messenger:

"You will bear a son."

"You will call him Ishmael."

"He will be..."

And that memory filled me with a peace no one could take away.

Because feeding my son was not just a function of the body. It was a declaration. A truth that needed no voice:

I am his mother.

Sarai knew it. Though she never admitted it. Though she never said it. Though she never looked directly at him.

I saw her hands tense when he reached for my breast. I saw her face harden when he fell asleep on me. I saw her gaze fade when he called me with sounds only a mother understands.

She carried him. She dressed him. She showed him. She demanded him.

But he sought me—as if his soul recognized the place where he had been heard before he was born.

And no custom, no law, no tradition, no agreement could change that.

Abram, for his part, looked at Ishmael with silent pride. He lifted him in his arms. Spoke to him in a deep voice. Walked with him among the animals. Presented him to the men of the camp as his son, his firstborn, his heir.

But when he looked at me, there was something else—something unspoken, something I could not name.

Respect. Perhaps gratitude. Perhaps guilt. Perhaps all three.

And so the years passed.

Ishmael grew between three worlds:

Abram's world, which he saw as his future.

Sarai's world, which saw him as comfort and wound.

My world, the only place where he was simply my son.

I watched him run between the tents—strong, fast, confident—as if the desert had adopted him from the first day.

And every time I looked at him, every time his laughter filled the camp, every time his shadow stretched across the sand, I remembered the well. I remembered the Voice. I remembered the Encounter.

And I knew that this child—my child—was not the fruit of pain, but of promise.

THE NIGHT OF THE PACT

Ishmael was thirteen years old when it happened. He was already strong, fast, restless—with his father's gaze and the heart of the desert.

I watched him grow the way one watches a young tree that already carries the shape of the greatness it will one day become.

That night I woke up for no reason. Not because of a noise. Not because of a dream. I simply opened my eyes and knew I had to step outside the tent.

The camp was silent. The stars shone with a clarity only the desert understands. The air was cold—not harsh, but a cold that smelled of stars, of silence, of revelation.

A cold that awakened the senses.

I walked a few steps. And then I saw him.

Abram stood in the distance, speaking to someone I could not see—yet whose presence filled the night as if the darkness itself were listening.

It was not the first time I had seen him like this. But that night, something was different.

Because now I knew who He was.

I had heard that Voice. I had seen that glow. I had felt that weight in the air. I had been called by my name.

And seeing Abram bow, seeing his face shine with reverent fear, seeing his hands tremble, I understood—without anyone explaining it:

It was God Himself. The God of the Messenger. The God who found me by the well. The God who named my son. The God who sees.

I stood there in silence—not approaching, not interrupting.

It was not my conversation. It was not my covenant.

But He was my God.

And with that certainty, I returned to my tent and fell asleep in peace.

THE NEXT DAY

At dawn, Abraham gathered the entire camp. His voice carried a firmness that only appears when a man has heard something greater than himself.

He looked at us one by one, as if ensuring no one would miss what he was about to say.

"From this day forward," he announced, "my wife will no longer be called Sarai. Her name will be Sarah. And my name will no longer be Abram, but Abraham."

A murmur rippled through the camp. A new name. A new destiny. A new identity.

And inside me, silently, I said:

Of course it is Him. The God who changes names. The God who told me what to call my son. The God who gives and takes away. The God who sees.

But Abraham was not finished.

His face tightened slightly, as if preparing to speak something difficult but necessary.

"And now," he continued, "every male shall be circumcised. It is the sign of the covenant between God and us."

The air left my chest… Not for me… For my son.

My hand instinctively reached toward the place where he slept, as if I could shield him from the future with a gesture.

Ishmael.

My child. My boy. My promise.

The thought of his pain pierced me like an arrow. I cried silently—not out of rebellion, not out of fear, but out of love.

Yet alongside the pain, there was something else:

A deep peace. A certainty from the desert. A Voice still echoing in my memory:

"He will be…"

If that God commanded it, it was for a reason. For something. Toward something.

I had obeyed the Messenger. Abraham obeyed the God of the Messenger. And now Ishmael would obey too.

That same day, my son was circumcised.

He cried—yes—as brave boys cry when the body breaks for a moment to make way for destiny.

But when I held him afterward, when his head rested on my chest, when his breathing softened, I knew it was not an act of pain.

It was a seal. A mark. A sign.

A door opening toward a future I could not see but that was already written.

And as I held him, while his body trembled with exhaustion, I whispered silently:

"You are Ishmael. God heard you before you were born. And He will continue to hear you."

THE THREE MEN

That day began like any other. The sun had barely risen when I was already grinding grain, preparing the flour for the day's bread.

Ishmael—now almost a man—ran between the tents with the energy of his thirteenth year.

I was leaning over the workbench when I heard Abraham's voice—a different voice, a voice he used only when something sacred was happening.

I stepped out of the tent to see what was happening. And there they were.

Three men.

The air around them held a faint glow, as if sunlight bent itself to touch them.

I don't know where they came from. We hadn't seen them approach. We hadn't heard footsteps. They were simply there—standing before Abraham, as if they had emerged from the air itself.

Abraham ran to them. He ran. The patriarch, the chief, the man who never rushed for anything—ran.

And bowed to the ground.

I stood still, my hands covered in flour, watching from the shadow of the tent.

They were not ordinary men. They did not walk like travelers. They did not look like merchants. They did not breathe like shepherds.

There was something about them— something I recognized instantly.

The same presence. The same stillness. The same silent authority I had felt in the wilderness when the Messenger called me by name.

Abraham spoke quickly, with that mixture of urgency and reverence only he possessed:

"My lord, if I have found favor in your eyes, do not pass by your servant. Let me bring water… wash your feet… rest under the tree…"

Then he called Sarah… Sarah, not me.

"Hurry!" he said.

"Take three measures of fine flour, knead it, and bake bread."

I listened from the entrance. I didn't move. It wasn't my place. It wasn't my order. It wasn't my moment.

But as Sarah kneaded the flour, I watched her.

Her hands trembled slightly—not from fatigue, but from something deeper, something she herself could not name.

I prepared other things—water, utensils, vessels—not because I was asked, but because it was my duty.

As I worked, I heard the voices outside. I couldn't make out the words, but I recognized the tone.

A tone I knew well—the tone of heaven speaking softly.

When I stepped out with the vessels, the three men sat under the tree, and Abraham served them meat, milk, and butter as if tending to kings.

I stood to the side, unseen, but seeing everything.

Then one of them spoke:

"Where is Sarah, your wife?"

The question fell upon the camp like a stone in a pond—silent, but sending ripples through every tent.

Sarah was inside, listening. Always listening. Always waiting for something that never came.

Abraham answered:

"She is in the tent."

And the man said:

"I will surely return to you… and Sarah will have a son."

The air stopped. Not from surprise. Not from disbelief.

From recognition.

It was the same Voice. The same authority. The same certainty that spoke to me by the well.

Sarah laughed—a bitter laugh, a laugh that said:

"That is not for me."

The laugh of a woman who has buried so much hope she no longer knows how to hold a new one.

And I understood her. Because I had laughed like that before He found me.

The men rose later, as if their visit had been only a whisper in time.

Abraham walked with them a few steps.

I watched from afar, my heart pounding.

I knew who they were. I knew what their visit meant. I knew something was about to change.

And as I put away the vessels, as I extinguished the fire, as the camp returned to its routine,

I thought:

"He has come again. But this time, He did not come for me. He came for her."

And though my heart tightened—not from envy, but from understanding—I also felt peace.

For the God who saw me in my affliction had now seen Sarah in hers.

And that—though no one knew it—was the beginning of the end.

THE INTERCESSION

When the three men rose to leave, I was still nearby—gathering the remains of the meal, washing the utensils, doing what I always did: serve in silence, watch in silence.

Abraham walked with them for a while, as he always did with important guests. But this time, there was something different in his posture.

He did not walk like a host. He walked like a man accompanying kings.

I watched them from a distance, the sun beating on their backs, the wind lifting small swirls of sand behind them.

Ishmael stood beside me—already tall, already strong, already carrying the shape of the man he would become. Every time I looked at him, I remembered the well, the Voice, the promise.

Thirteen years. Thirteen years since He spoke to me. Thirteen years since He called me by my name. Thirteen years since He told me who my son would be.

And every year that passed, every inch Ishmael grew, was a silent reminder that God does not forget.

Abraham was ninety-nine years old. I watched him walk—slow, but steady—as if age weighed not on his bones, but on his memories.

The three men stopped. Abraham stopped with them. I could not hear their words, but I could see their gestures, their faces, the gravity in the air.

Something was happening. Something big. Something not meant for my ears, but that my eyes could read between the lines.

One of the men stayed with Abraham. The other two continued toward the valley.

I stepped forward—just enough to see, not enough to be seen.

Abraham's face changed.

It tightened.

It softened.

It brightened and darkened at the same time.

And then I heard it—not everything, just fragments carried by the wind:

"Sodom…" "Outcry…" "Destruction…"

Then Abraham's voice—trembling, yet firm:

"Will You indeed sweep away the righteous with the wicked…"

I froze. I had never heard Abraham speak like that. It was not pleading. It was not fear. It was something deeper: intercession.

As if he were fighting for someone he loved. As if he were negotiating with heaven itself.

The Man answered. I could not hear the words, but I recognized the tone. A tone I knew. A tone I had heard in the desert. A tone that left no doubt.

It was Him. The same God who saw me. The same God who spoke to me. The same God who promised me Ishmael.

Abraham insisted. Once. Again. Again.

Fifty. Forty-five. Forty. Thirty. Twenty. Ten.

The wind seemed to stop each time he spoke—as if the desert itself were listening to the negotiation.

I did not understand everything, but I understood enough:

Abraham was fighting for lives that were not his. For cities that were not his. For people who were not his.

And the God who saw me listened to him.

When the conversation ended, the Man departed. Abraham returned to the camp with tired shoulders and eyes carrying a weight he shared with no one.

I watched him from afar—watched him pause before entering his tent, as if he needed one breath to return to being the man everyone knew.

Ishmael approached me.

"What happened?" he asked.

I looked at him—my son, my promise, my future.

"Something great," I said.

"Something you won't understand today. But one day you will."

He ran off toward the boys in the camp. I looked toward the horizon.

Because although no one knew it, although no one suspected it, although no one asked,

I understood something that pierced my soul: The God who saw me in my affliction also sees the cities. He sees the righteous. He sees the wicked. He hears the outcry.

And that night, while the camp slept, I remembered my own encounter, my own cry, my own well.

And I knew…

…that the God who hears

…does not change.

THE GOD WHO DEVASTATES

The news reached the camp three days later. Not through Abraham. Not through Sarah. Not through official messengers.

It came the way all unwanted news arrives: through the women.

I was grinding grain when I heard the whispers—first timid, as if the words burned the tongue, then stronger, as if fear needed to escape before suffocating the one who carried it.

"They say Sodom no longer exists…"

"They say Gomorrah was swallowed by fire…"

"They say the whole valley smells of sulfur…"

"They say nothing is left… nothing…"

Abraham's shepherds had returned that morning. Their faces said everything before their words confirmed it.

I approached slowly—not interrupting, not showing too much interest. A servant learns to listen without being seen.

"They say fire fell from the sky," one whispered.

"They say it was the God of Abraham," said another.

"They say He decided it Himself," a third added.

A chill ran down my spine. Not because of the news. Because of recognition.

The God who spoke to me in the wilderness.

The God who saw me cry by the well.

The God who promised me Ishmael.

The God who heard my affliction—that same God had destroyed entire cities.

I stood still, my hands in the flour, my eyes fixed on a single point in the sand.

The smell of flour on my hands mixed with an imagined scent of distant smoke—as if my body understood before my mind did.

It was not fear. Not exactly. It was something deeper—something I did not know how to name then, but that now, after many years, I can say clearly:

reverence and fear.

Because I understood something no one had ever explained to me:

The God who sees also judges. The God who hears also responds. The God who promises also demands. The God who saves also devastates.

And that truth pierced my soul.

Ishmael was thirteen. Every time I looked at him, I remembered the promise. I remembered the Voice. I remembered the Messenger.

But now, as I heard of Sodom, I understood something else:

The God who promised me a future could also take everything away in an instant.

Not on a whim. Not out of cruelty. But because He is God. Truly God. Almighty God. A God who does not bend to culture, to human morality, or to the limits of understanding.

A God who feels. A God who grieves. A God who is angered. A God who acts.

That afternoon, as the camp murmured, as the women repeated stories, as the men spoke in low voices, I remained silent.

I watched Ishmael run between the tents—strong, fast, alive.

And I thought:

"The God who destroyed Sodom is the same God who saw me. The same God who heard my cry. The same God who promised my son a future."

And for the first time in my life, I felt something I had not felt even in the desert:

holy fear… Not terror. Not dread. Not anguish.

Holy fear—a gentle trembling born not of fright, but of the recognition that one stands before a real, living, powerful, deeply sensitive God. A God who responds to human behavior.

And that night, while the camp slept, while the wind carried a distant scent of smoke, while the sky seemed darker than usual, I prayed in silence.

Not to ask… Not to complain… Not to demand.

But simply to say:

"You saw me. You heard me. You promised me. And I fear You. And I believe You."

THE GOD WHO CLOSES AND OPENS

I do not know how many years had passed since the Messenger spoke to me in the wilderness. Perhaps fourteen. Perhaps a little more.

Ishmael was already tall—with the strength of a young man and the restless gaze of someone discovering the world.

Abraham was ninety-nine years old. His body was old, but his spirit was not. There was an energy in him that came not from age, but from the covenant.

One day, without warning, Abraham ordered us to break camp. He did not explain why. He did not say where we were going. He simply said:

"We move toward Gerar."

And when Abraham spoke like that, no one asked questions.

I gathered my things, as always. Ishmael helped me, as always.

Sarah walked in silence, as she almost always did.

But there was something on her face—a tension, a shadow, a restlessness she could not hide.

We arrived in Gerar. A strange place—neither hostile nor welcoming. Just… different.

And then it happened.

Abimelech, the king of the land, saw Sarah.

And he took her.

Just like that. As if it were customary. As if it were lawful. As if it were nothing.

I saw it. I saw her being escorted out of the camp. I saw Abraham lower his head. I saw Sarah say nothing.

And inside me, something broke.

Not out of jealousy. Not out of rivalry. Not out of competition.

Out of recognition.

Because I knew what it was like to be taken. I knew what it was like to have no voice. I knew what it was like for your body to become someone else's decision.

That night, the camp was restless. The men murmured. The women speculated. Ishmael asked me what was happening.

I did not know what to tell him.

But Abraham… Abraham was different. He did not eat. He did not speak. He did not sleep.

He paced back and forth like a man awaiting judgment.

And I watched him from afar—not approaching, not interrupting, not asking.

Because there was something in his face I had seen before.

I had seen it in myself when the Messenger spoke to me by the well. I had seen it in him when he interceded for Sodom.

It was the face of someone who knows God is about to intervene.

And so it was.

The next morning, Abimelech returned Sarah. He had not touched her. He had not harmed her. He had not humiliated her.

He returned her—with gifts, with apologies, with fear. And he said something I will never forget:

"Your God spoke to me last night."

A chill ran through me.

Not from surprise.

From recognition.

God Himself. The God of the Messenger. The God who saw me. The God who hears. The God who judges. The God who destroyed Sodom. The God who protects Sarah.

That God had closed the wombs of Abimelech's household. That God had stopped the king's hand. That God had returned Sarah intact.

And while the women murmured, while the men discussed the restitution, while Sarah remained silent, I understood something that pierced my soul:

The God who saw me also saw her.

The God who promised me Ishmael was also preparing the way for Isaac.

The God who called me by name was also about to call Sarah's son by name.

And that night, while the camp slept, while the wind moved through the tents, while Ishmael breathed deeply beside me,

I thought:

"He closes

…He opens

…He takes

…He returns

…He judges

…He saves…He sees."

…And I knew something great was coming.

THE CHANGE IN SARA

The days after our stay in Gerar were strange. Not because of the journey. Not because of the weather. Not because of the movement of the camp.

But because of Sarah.

There was something different about her—something I did not know how to name at first, but that my eyes, trained to read silences, could not ignore.

Ever since Abraham announced that her name would no longer be Sarai, but Sarah, I had noticed a slight change—like a light turning on behind a curtain. But after Gerar…that light began to grow.

Sarah walked differently. No longer bent by bitterness. No longer rigid with frustration. No longer strained by sterility. Her steps were firmer. Her back straighter. Her gaze more alive.

And her face… her face looked younger.

Not young like a girl, but young like a woman renewed from within—as if the change of name had also been a change of destiny, a change of body, a change of soul.

I watched her from afar—not intruding, not asking, not disturbing.

Because among women, there are things understood without words.

The bitterness that once escaped her lips slowly faded—like a fire running out of wood. And in its place, something appeared I had never seen in her:

joy.

A shy joy, almost hidden, as if she feared it might break if she showed it too openly.

I was cautious. Not out of suspicion—but out of experience.

One day, while grinding grain, I saw her stop mid-motion. She placed her hand on her belly with a gesture I knew too well.

Her fingers trembled slightly—as if her body knew before she did that something new was beginning.

That gesture. That touch. That instinctive caress a woman makes when she feels life inside her.

My heart skipped a beat. Not from envy. Not from pain. Not from jealousy.

From joy.

For if the God who met me in the wilderness—the God who spoke to me by the well, the God who promised me Ishmael, the God who saw me weep—if that God could cause a barren old woman to conceive and give birth… then that God was greater than I had imagined.

More powerful.

More mysterious.

More intimate.

More near.

I watched her for a moment, unseen. And inside me, without speaking it aloud, I thought:

"He saw her too."

And that certainty—that understanding—that silent revelation—filled me with a peace I did not expect.

Because I understood something that changed my heart:

The God who promised me a son was not only the God of slaves. He was also the God of free women.

The God of the old.

The God of the barren.

The God of impossibilities.

The God who sees.

And as Sarah walked on, touching her belly with that mixture of fear and hope, I smiled.

Because I knew something great was coming—something that would change the camp, change history, change my life and my son's.

And though no one told me, though no one announced it, though no one confessed it,

I knew:

Sarah was pregnant.

And in that moment, I felt heaven open two paths— one for her…

….and one for me.

Chapter 10

"THE HEIR SON"

The Birth of the Promised Son

On the day Isaac was born, the entire camp woke with a different air. I cannot explain it. It wasn't a sound. It wasn't an announcement.

It was… a vibration. As if the earth itself knew that something was about to break open and be born.

I was grinding grain, as always, when I heard the first scream.

The air inside the tent trembled, as if the desert recognized that sound and returned it amplified.

It was not an ordinary cry of pain. It was a deep, ancient cry—the cry of a woman who has waited a lifetime to feel what she was feeling.

Sarah.

I froze, my hands suspended over the flour. Not from surprise. From recognition.

Because I knew that sound. I had screamed like that. I had felt that tearing. I had lived that mixture of pain and glory when Ishmael left my body and made me a mother.

The women ran to Sarah's tent. I did not go. It was not my place. Not my space. Not my story.

But I stayed close—close enough to hear, far enough not to be seen.

The screams grew stronger. Then shorter. Then deeper. And then… a brief silence, like a sigh from heaven.

And then I heard it.

A cry.

A cry that pierced the camp like an arrow of light, breaking decades of silence in Sarah's womb.

Small. New. Fragile. But full of life. The cry of a child.

Isaac's cry.

Something inside me moved. It was not envy. Not pain. Not jealousy.

It was… astonishment.

Because I knew what that cry meant. I knew what that birth represented. I knew this child was not just a son.

He was a promise. A word made flesh. A miracle that had taken decades to arrive.

The women emerged from the tent with shining eyes. Some cried. Some laughed. Some whispered blessings.

I stood still, watching from the shadows, as always.

And then I saw her.

Sarah stepped out, supported by two women—but her face glowed as I had never seen it before.

She held the child in her arms.

Her hands trembled slightly, as if she were holding not only a son but a promise she had waited too long to touch.

She looked at him as if he were the first light in the world—as if all her pain, all her waiting, all her bitterness, all her sterility had been erased in an instant.

And I understood.

The God who saw me in the wilderness had also seen her. The God who promised me Ishmael had also promised her a son. The God who gave me a future had also given her a beginning.

Abraham arrived shortly after. His eyes filled with tears—not of sadness, but of something deeper, something only a hundred-year-old man can feel when he holds a miracle in his arms.

He lifted the child.

He kissed him.

The sound of that kiss was soft—but heavy with the weight of a century of waiting.

He called him by name: Isaac. Laughter. Joy. Promise kept.

Ishmael stood beside me—fourteen years old, tall, strong, beautiful.

My son.

My promise.

I looked at him. And as he gazed curiously at the newborn, I felt something unexpected:

peace.

A warm peace, like water running over a tired stone.

Because I understood that Isaac's birth did not erase Ishmael's promise. It did not cancel it. It did not diminish it.

The God who opens wombs does not close destinies.

And while the camp celebrated, while the women sang, while Abraham laughed, while Sarah wept with joy, I remained silent, my heart full.

Because I knew that not only Isaac had been born that day.

That day, the beginning of the end was born.

But also the beginning of something greater than any of us could imagine.

THE MARK IN THE FLESH

On the day Isaac was circumcised, the entire camp moved with a different solemnity.

It was not a celebration.

It was not mourning.

It was something in between—a mixture of joy and awe, of celebration and reverence.

I knew what was coming.

The camp smelled of wood smoke and fresh oil, as if the earth itself were preparing for a sacred act.

I had seen it before. I had lived it before. I had felt it in my own son.

Ishmael was fourteen when he was circumcised. I still remember his face—the mixture of courage and pain, the way he squeezed my hands, the way his breath trembled as Abraham carried out the command of the God of the covenant.

That day, as I prepared clean water and cloth, I looked at Isaac—so small, so fragile, so new to the world.

And I thought:

"He will also carry the mark."

The mark of the covenant. The mark of the God who saw me. The mark of the God who hears. The mark of the God who demands. The mark of the God who promises.

Abraham stepped out of his tent with Isaac in his arms. His hands trembled slightly—not from fear, but from reverence.

Sarah walked behind him, her face tense, but her eyes filled with a light she had never carried before. The light of a mother who knows her son is entering a destiny greater than herself.

I stood aside, as always—not intervening, not approaching, but seeing everything.

Abraham performed the rite.

The silence that followed was so profound it felt like an invisible seal falling upon history.

I did not hear the child's cry, but I saw Sarah's gesture—the way she pressed her lips together, the way her hands tightened around her cloak.

When it was over, Abraham placed Isaac in her arms. She received him with a mixture of pride and pain—as if that small cut were also a cut in her own soul.

I returned to my tent.

Ishmael sat there, cleaning a bowstring, as if nothing important were happening.

But I knew he remembered. I saw it in his eyes.

I sat beside him.

“Today Isaac received the sign,” I said.

He nodded, still working.

“Like me,” he answered.

His voice carried a tone that was not pride and not pain—but memory.

“Yes,” I said softly.

“Like you.”

I was silent for a moment. Then I added:

“That sign is not just a rite. It is a mark. A door. A way of telling God that you belong to Him and that He hears you.”

Ishmael looked up. His eyes carried the depth of the desert.

“And when I have sons?” he asked.

My heart filled—not with nostalgia,but with hope.

“When you have sons,” I said, “you will circumcise them too. Because that sign is not only for you. It is for your descendants—for those who will come after you. So they too may speak to the God who heard you before you were born.”

Ishmael said nothing. But his silence was not empty. It was a silence that thought. A silence that understood. A silence that received.

I looked at him—my son, my promise, my future.

And inside me, without speaking it aloud, I thought:

"The mark is in his flesh, but the covenant is in his destiny."

That afternoon, as the camp quieted, as Isaac slept in Sarah's arms, as Abraham meditated in silence, I felt something I had not felt since the well:

certainty.

The God who saw me continued writing stories in the flesh of men—stories that could not be erased, stories that would pass from father to son, from son to grandson, from generation to generation.

And I knew that Ishmael—my son, my boy, my promise—would carry that story wherever the desert called him.

THE WEANING PARTY

On the day of Isaac's weaning feast, the entire camp moved with unusual energy.

The aroma of freshly baked bread mixed with the sweet scent of roasted meat, creating an atmosphere of celebration that could be felt even before the laughter began.

Abraham had ordered a great banquet—and when Abraham commanded such a thing, we all knew it was an important day.

Isaac was two, perhaps three years old—a small child, still fragile, but full of that light that only long-awaited children carry. He walked awkwardly, babbling words, laughing easily.

And everyone celebrated.

Everyone…

…Except one

…Ishmael.

THE HEIR SON

My son was sixteen or seventeen—a strong, tall young man, his muscles shaped by desert work, his gaze restless, his spirit eager to take on the world.

He was fast, agile, brave—and sometimes…too sure of himself.

I saw him from afar. I saw the way he looked at Isaac. I saw his brow tighten. I saw his jaw clench.

And I understood.

It was the gaze of a young man watching the world reorganize itself without asking his permission.

It was not hatred. It was not malice. It was something deeper:

displacement.

For the first time in his life, Ishmael was not the center. Not the only child. Not the heir. Not the future.

He was… the older one. The previous one. The one who came before the miracle.

And for a young man full of strength, that is a hard truth to swallow.

As the men laughed, as the women sang, as Abraham lifted Isaac in his arms, I saw Ishmael make a gesture.

A laugh. A smirk. A comment I could not hear—but whose tone I recognized instantly.

It was the laughter of a young man who feels superior. The laughter of someone who looks at a small child and thinks: "This one? This is the heir?"

My heart tightened.

Not for Isaac. Not for Sarah… For Ishmael.

Because I knew that laugh—that mockery—that attitude—was not a game.

It was an omen.

I approached him. Not angry. Not shouting. With the authority that only a mother who has seen God can carry.

"Ishmael," I said softly. "Don't do that."

He looked at me with that mixture of pride and confusion that only the young possess.

"I was just playing," he said.

"No," I answered. "You weren't playing. You were mocking. And that is not right."

My voice trembled slightly—not from fear, but from the weight of what I knew was coming.

He frowned.

"Why? He's just a child."

"Because that child," I said, "is also the son of the God who heard you. The God who spoke to me in the wilderness. The God who promised you a future. The God who gave you a name before you were born."

Ishmael lowered his gaze.

His shadow stretched across the sand—as if his heart had aged a year in a single breath. Not from shame. From understanding.

"You bear the mark of the covenant," I continued. "And one day, when you have sons, you will circumcise them too. Because that mark is not only yours. It belongs to your descendants. It belongs to your story. It belongs to your destiny."

He inhaled deeply—his chest rising with the strength of a young man learning to become a man.

"Isaac is not your enemy," I said. "Nor your replacement. Nor your shadow. He is part of the plan of the God who heard you first."

Ishmael looked up.

His eyes carried a glimmer that was not anger. It was pain. And behind the pain—understanding.

I embraced him. Not as a servant. Not as a rival. As a mother.

And as I held him, while the feast continued around us, while Isaac laughed in Abraham's arms, I knew something that pierced my soul:

The conflict had begun. And nothing could stop what was coming.

But I also knew something else—a certainty bitter and luminous at the same time:

The God who saw me does not abandon the children of promise, even when their paths diverge.

The God who saw me in the wilderness would continue to see my son in everything that was to come.

Chapter 11

"THE FAREWELL"

The Day We Left The Camp

The weaning feast had ended hours earlier. The camp was silent—but not a peaceful silence. It was a tense silence, the kind that settles over the earth before a storm breaks.

I was putting away the last vessels when I heard the sound I did not want to hear:

Sarah's voice.

It was not a scream. It was not a cry. It was worse.

It was that cold, sharp tone she only used when something inside her had shattered or ignited.

I hid behind the fabric of my tent—not out of cowardice, but because I knew that conversation was not meant for my ears.

But still… I listened.

"Throw out that servant and her son!"

The air inside the tent thickened, as if even the wind refused to move those words.

My heart stopped.

She did not say my name.

She did not say Hagar.

She said: "That servant."

As if I were an object. A nuisance. A shadow. And then she added the words that pierced my soul:

"For the son of that servant shall not inherit with my son Isaac."

The world shrank around me. Not for me. For Ishmael…

My son.

My boy.

My promise.

I heard Abraham answer. His voice was broken—not with anger, but with pain.

"Sarah… don't ask for that…"

Then came a long silence. A silence that hurt. A silence that said more than any words could.

That silence fell on me like a stone—reminding me that sometimes love does not know how to defend.

I knew what that silence meant.

Abraham was torn—between his wife and his son, between duty and heart, between her promise and mine.

And I… I was in the middle, unable to move, unable to speak, unable to defend myself.

Like that time in Egypt. Like that time in the wilderness. Like so many times before.

The night deepened. The voices faded. The shadows lengthened.

I returned to my tent, but sleep did not come.

THE FAREWELL

Ishmael slept soundly—unaware of everything, with the peace of a young man who does not know his world is about to break.

I watched him for a long time. His chest rising and falling. His face relaxed. His hand resting on his bow.

That bow—symbol of his future strength—looked as fragile as he did in that moment.

And I… I felt something I had not felt in years: fear.

An ancient fear. A fear I knew too well. A fear I thought I had left behind when the Messenger found me by the well.

I lay beside him, but sleep did not come. My mind raced. My heart trembled. My soul shrank.

I thought of Sarah. I thought of Abraham. I thought of Isaac. I thought of Ishmael.

And I thought of Him—the God who sees, the God who hears, the God who promises, the God who saves.

But that night… He felt far away.

Not because He had left—but because fear made me feel as if I were returning to the wilderness of uncertainty.

I covered myself with my cloak and closed my eyes.

And in the darkness, with my heart pounding, I whispered silently:

"If You see me…

…if You still see me…

…do not abandon me now."

And so I fell asleep—not in peace, not in calm, but in that bitter mixture of doubt and hope known only to those who have been saved once and fear falling again.

THE MORNING OF THE NAME

The morning after the weaning feast dawned like any other.

The sun touched the tents. The animals stirred. The women began their tasks.

And I… I tried to convince myself that the night before had only been a bad dream.

I woke early, as always. Fetched water. Lit the fire. Ground the grain. Straightened the tent. Everything the same. Everything normal.

But inside me, something was out of place.

There was a weight in the air. A strange silence. A sensation I could not name—but my body recognized it.

And then I heard it. My name.

"Hagar."

Not "servant." Not "you." Not "she." My name.

Abraham's voice.

His voice trembled slightly—as if each syllable weighed more than he could carry.

My heart raced. Not because it was a kind call. But because Abraham almost never called me that.

THE FAREWELL

When he spoke my name, it meant something great, something serious, something irrevocable was about to happen.

I turned slowly. And I saw him.

Abraham was walking toward me. But he was not alone. Beside him was Ishmael—my son, my boy, my promise.

And in Abraham's hands…

A wineskin… And bread.

A skin of water—flexible, full. The same kind of container I carried when I fled into the wilderness seventeen years earlier.

My breath stopped.

Abraham approached. His face was tense—but not hard. There was pain in his eyes. Real pain. A father's pain. The pain of a divided man.

He stopped before me. He looked at me.

And for a moment, I saw the same man who received me when I returned pregnant, the same man who circumcised my son, the same man who interceded for Sodom.

But now… now he came with an order.

An order that was not his. An order from above.

He extended the wineskin.

The leather was warm from the sun—but in my hands it felt cold, like an omen.

And he said:

"Hagar… you must leave the camp. You and your son. You cannot stay here."

THE FAREWELL

The world moved beneath my feet. I did not cry. I did not scream. I did not speak.

I simply listened.

Abraham took a deep breath.

"God will be with you," he said. "This… this has been approved by Him."

His words were a double-edged blade—they wounded, but they also held me upright.

Approved by God.

The same God who found me in the wilderness. The same God who called me by name. The same God who promised me Ishmael. The same God who saw me cry by the well.

That God had approved my expulsion.

A storm of emotions hit me at once:

Surprise. Pain. Confusion. Anger. Fear. And beneath them all—a spark of faith I did not know whether to embrace or reject.

I took the wineskin with trembling hands. I looked at Ishmael. He did not understand—not yet. But his eyes searched mine, like when he was a child and I feared the dark.

I wanted to tell him everything would be well. I wanted to tell him God would see us again. I wanted to tell him the promise was still alive.

But I couldn't.

Not that morning.

Abraham lowered his gaze—not from shame, but from pain.

And I…I stood there, wineskin in hand, my son beside me, my heart in pieces, wondering how the same God who saved me was now sending me back into the wilderness.

And as the sun rose, as the camp awakened, as life continued as if nothing had happened, I knew that my safety, my home, my destiny, my story…

…were about to break once again.

THE CRY OF THE DESERT

The desert has a weight. The air smelled of hot dust, and every breath felt like a warning that there would be no easy return.

It is not just sand. It is not just sun. It is a weight that falls on the shoulders, on the chest, on the soul.

And that day, when Abraham sent us away, I felt that weight from the very first step.

We walked without direction. There was no destination. No plan. Only a skin of water, a piece of bread, and a son who was no longer a boy but not yet a man.

Ishmael walked in silence. His face was hardened—not with anger, but with questions, with wounds, with the confusion of youth that cannot understand why the world collapses without warning.

I watched him from the corner of my eye. I saw his breathing grow heavier. I saw his pace slow. I saw his gaze drift toward the horizon, as if searching for answers I could not give him.

The sun fell mercilessly. Each hour longer than the last. Each step heavier. Each sip of water smaller.

And inside me, something began to break.

THE FAREWELL

Another sending away. Another escape. The desert again. Uncertainty again.

The old feeling of being discarded—the woman who is left over, the woman who gets in the way, the woman who is abandoned.

The old shadows returned: Vulnerability. Contempt. Loneliness. Fear.

And with each step, each drop of sweat, each sip of water that evaporated before reaching the throat, those shadows grew.

Until the moment I feared arrived.

The water was gone.

Not a drop left.

Not a hope.

Not a strength.

Ishmael stopped. His breathing was ragged—each exhale a lament trying not to become a cry.

His skin burned. His lips cracked. His eyes… His eyes carried a gleam that tore me apart: the gleam of abandonment.

Not because I wanted to abandon him—but because the desert was taking our lives.

I took his arm.

I led him to a dry bush—the only shade in sight. A small, brittle bush, insufficient for such a destiny.

I placed him there, like a mother tending a sick child, even though he was almost a man.

And then something happened I never thought possible:

I could not bear it.

I could not watch him die. I could not watch life slip from him. I could not watch the son of promise fade before my eyes.

I walked away. Not far. Just far enough not to see him. Just far enough not to hear his last breath.

Each step was a tear—as if my feet were being torn from the earth that held my son.

And as I walked away, I felt something that broke me more than the sun, more than thirst, more than the desert:

Ishmael felt I was abandoning him.

I saw it in his eyes. I heard it in his breathing. I sensed it in his silence.

First his father.

Now his mother.

The boy who had always been strong, always brave, always proud…

broke.

And in that breaking, in that pain, in that absolute loneliness—he remembered. He remembered what I told him about the Messenger.

He remembered the promise. He remembered the God who sees. He remembered the God who named him before he was born.

And then, for the first time in his life, Ishmael did what I had done seventeen years earlier:

He cried.

Not a whisper. Not a timid prayer. Not a thought.

A scream.

A cry full of pain. A cry full of fear. A cry full of abandonment. A cry full of life.

A cry that seemed to split the sky in two—as if the entire desert had become an altar.

A cry that crossed the wilderness like a flaming arrow.

A cry that was not for me. Not for Abraham. Not for Sarah.

It was for Him.

For the God who sees. For the God who hears. For the God who promises. For the God who saves.

And as his voice rose—broken, strong, desperate—I knew that cry would not be lost in the wind.

THE VOICE THAT BREAKS THE SKY

Ishmael's cry still vibrated in the air as the desert fell silent—a silence so deep it felt as if the world held its breath.

I was on my knees, my face in my hands, crying in silence, convinced my story had ended there—under the relentless sun, among sands that had seen me fall so many times.

And then it happened.

A voice.

Not a whisper. Not a wind. Not a thought.

A voice.

THE FAREWELL

It did not descend—it fell, like rain that does not ask permission to touch the earth.

Strong. Powerful. Alive. As if heaven had opened and eternity itself had decided to speak.

And it said:

"What is it, Hagar?"

My name. My name again. Not spoken by a man. Not by a messenger. Not by a dream.

By heaven itself.

I turned immediately. I searched desperately. I looked around, hoping to see the Messenger—the man who found me by the well seventeen years ago.

But no one was there.

The voice did not come from the earth. It did not come from the horizon. It did not come from a man.

It came from above.

And that shook me more than the sun, more than thirst, more than fear.

It was as if God Himself was speaking to me.

I wanted to answer. I wanted to tell Him I was broken, tired, confused—that I had stopped believing, that I feared my chaotic destiny was stronger than His promise.

But before I could speak, the voice continued:

"Do not be afraid."

Those words pierced me like fresh water. They entered me like cold water into a fevered body.

“Do not be afraid.”

It was not a scolding. Not a judgment. It was… a Father.

A Father who sees His daughter trembling and says:

“I am here.”

And then He added:

“For God has heard the voice of the boy where he is.”

When I heard that, something inside me broke and rebuilt at the same time.

He had not only seen me… He had not only heard me.

He had heard my son.

My son—the boy I thought was lost, the boy I left under a bush, the boy who screamed like someone calling a father.

God had heard him.

And before I could cry, or thank, or fall to the ground—the voice spoke again:

“Get up. Lift up the boy with your hand, for I will make him a great nation.”

It was not a suggestion. Not a consolation. It was an order.

An order that gave me my life back. An order that reminded me of my purpose. An order that said:

“Be a mother. Be strong. Be his guide. Your son is not destined to die. He is destined to rise.”

And in that instant, I understood something I had never fully understood:

It was not just about carrying him. It was about training him. Teaching him. Strengthening him. Preparing him to be a leader, a prince, a nation.

And then, as if heaven wished to seal its words, I lifted my eyes…

and I saw water.

A brightness so intense it looked like an open eye in the middle of the desert.

A fountain. A well. The same kind of well where the Messenger found me years ago.

I do not know if it had always been there or if it appeared in that moment. I do not know if my eyes were blind or if God opened them.

I only know that I saw it. And when I saw it, hope returned.

The desert was no longer a tomb. It was a road. A promise. A destiny.

And I understood something else:

The story of the despised woman was over.

The story written by God was the one that would prevail.

I rose.

I wiped my face.

I took a deep breath.

And I walked toward my son with a determination I had never felt before.

Because I was no longer the broken Hagar. Nor the sent-away Hagar. Nor the abandoned Hagar.

I was the Hagar called by God. Strengthened by His voice. Destined to raise a prince. To raise a nation.

And as I walked toward him, I understood:

The wilderness was not my end. It was my silent coronation.

And nothing—and no one—would ever again change the purpose God had declared over our lives.

Chapter 12

"THE ETERNAL RIDE"

The Farewell to Eternity

I had finished repairing the crack in the well. My hands—now old—moved with the same delicacy with which a mother adjusts a sleeping child.

That well had been my companion, my witness, my altar, my memory.

I sat beside it, as I had done for years, and rested my palm on the warm stone.

The stone held an ancient warmth, as if it still remembered all my tears.

"That is the whole story, dear friend," I said.

"Everything I lived… everything I cried… everything I learned…"

The wind blew softly, as if the desert itself were listening.

And then I felt it.

A shadow. Not a cloud. Not a tree. A presence.

A shadow that did not darken, but protected. A shadow that did not cool, but embraced. A shadow that brought peace.

The air around me grew denser, as if the Presence itself were breathing with me.

I closed my eyes—not out of fear, but out of desire.

Because when one wants to feel God, sometimes it is better to turn off the eyes to ignite the soul.

And in that silence, in that stillness, in that light that did not come from the sun,

I heard the Voice.

It was not sound—it was existence. It was as if the universe pronounced my name from its root.

Not the voice of the Messenger. Not the wind. Not memory.

The Voice.

The same Voice that called me in the wilderness. The same Voice that heard my son. The same Voice that opened the well.

And it said:

"Hagar."

My name fell upon me like a blanket of light—soft and heavy at the same time.

My name. My name again. Spoken with tenderness, with authority, with eternity.

"Everything I told you in the past has come to pass. And everything that remains will be fulfilled. For I am not a man to lie."

My eyes filled with tears—not of sadness, but of recognition, of love, of certainty.

It was as if every promise I had guarded in silence ignited within me.

The Voice continued:

THE ETERNAL RIDE

"The time has come for you to walk with Me to the place I have prepared for you."

My heart opened like a flower in the rain.

Joy.

…Peace

…Rest

…A release

…I had not known for decades.

I opened my eyes.

And there he was. The Messenger.

The same. Exactly the same.

His presence had not aged. It was the same radiance I had seen when I was young and fleeing.

Beautiful. Radiant. Unchanging. As if time could not touch him. As if eternity wrapped around him.

He smiled—that smile that knew my wounds and my victories. That smile that had seen the young slave girl and now saw the old matriarch.

He extended his hand.

I did not hesitate. I had never doubted him. I had never doubted that hand.

I took it.

His touch was warm—not like fire, but like dawn. And when I touched him, I felt my body, my soul, my story, my entire existence unite with that light.

It was as if my whole life was gathered into a single heartbeat—perfect and complete.

It was not death.

It was return. It was home. It was fulfillment.

I sighed—a sigh full of peace, a sigh that closed a cycle, a sigh that gave everything.

And together, the Messenger and I walked toward the horizon of the desert.

My steps did not hurt

…My back was not heavy

...My heart did not tremble.

I walked with him like one walks with an old friend. Like one returning home. Like one who no longer belongs to the earth.

The desert before us seemed to open—not as a path, but as a door.

And we walked on until we were no longer seen.

And in that final step, I knew:

The woman who once fled…

…now entered eternity accompanied.

Chapter 13

"THE OTHER ENCOUNTER"

The Return from Cairo to New York

Eliana finished reading the last line of the parchment.

The scroll cracked softly between her fingers, as if it too were exhaling after telling its story.

Her hands trembled. Her breath shortened. The desert sun was beginning to fall, painting the sand in shades of copper and fire.

She closed her eyes for a moment, as if she needed to absorb what she had just lived.

And when she opened them… something had changed.

The air grew denser. More alive. More sacred.

A light appeared around her. Not lightning. Not reflection. A light with weight. With presence. With voice.

The air vibrated, as if the sand itself recognized who was descending.

And that Voice called her by name: "Eliana."

Her name fell on her like an embrace she had waited for all her life.

She froze. Her heart pounded. Tears rose without permission.

The Voice continued:

THE OTHER ENCOUNTER

"I am Jesus. I am the Messenger of God. The same One who spoke with Hagar. The same One who accompanied her in the wilderness. The same One who inspired the author of The Mountain. And the same One who inspired you to come here."

His voice carried a tone that cannot be described—as if each word held a dawn inside it.

Eliana fell to her knees. Not out of fear. Out of recognition. Out of love. Out of the certainty that this Voice had been searching for her for years.

Tears streamed down her face—not tears of sorrow, but tears that washed, that healed, that freed.

Each tear carried a memory. Each tear uprooted an old wound. Each tear loosened a weight she had carried too long.

The Voice spoke again:

"I know everything you have suffered. I know what you are running from. I know what hurts you. But I have come to strengthen you. To lift you up. Do not fear. You are not alone. I am with you always."

Those words touched places inside her she did not know were still open.

Eliana pressed the parchment to her chest. She felt something inside her being rebuilt—as if her soul were being assembled again, piece by piece, by divine hands.

The Voice continued:

"When you feel despised, speak to Me—for I will embrace you. When you feel worthless, speak to Me—for I will remind you how precious you are to Me."

Eliana sobbed—but this time it was not pain. It was birth.

And then the Voice said something that stole her breath:

"Eliana…you carry life within you. And that child will have a great purpose. Care for him. Teach him. Train him as one trains a leader. Show him My ways. Tell him about Me. For he will be a blessing to many."

Eliana placed her hands on her belly.

Her fingers trembled as she felt a warmth that did not come from her body, but from a promise. A gentle warmth. A pulse. A certainty.

And in that instant, she understood Hagar. She understood her story. She understood her pain. She understood her promise.

The light began to fade, as if heaven were slowly closing a door. The air carried a faint fragrance, as if the Presence had left an invisible mark.

The desert returned to silence. The sunset wrapped her in shadow.

And then she heard human voices:

"Miss! Miss! The bus is ready!"

It was the driver. The engine was running. The journey to Sinai would continue.

Eliana said nothing. She looked at the parchment. She stroked it one last time. Then she buried it again in the sand—in the same place where she had found it. The sand fell over it like a seal, as if the desert were claiming it back into its eternal memory.

It was not hers. It belonged to the desert. It belonged to Hagar. It belonged to the story.

THE OTHER ENCOUNTER

Weeks later, back in New York, Eliana was no longer the woman who had fled. She was not the broken woman. She was not the hiding woman. She was a woman marked by a promise. A woman who walked with purpose. A woman who carried a sacred secret in her womb and in her soul.

The city greeted her with its usual noise—but inside her there was a new silence, a silence full of purpose.

And one afternoon, while waiting tables, she saw him.

The clinking of cutlery faded. Time paused.

The man from the book… The elegant man. The man who had placed The Mountain in her hands without explanation.

He looked at her… He smiled… And he said:

"Sit down. Tell me what you experienced. Because I must write it."

Eliana sat. She took a deep breath. And she began to speak.

And that man…

…he wrote her story.

…and that man…

…is me.

And I wrote what you have just read. Because some stories are not simply read—they are received. And they transcend time, space, and matter.

And this one…

…this one was hers.

A Hidden Wound Can Never Be Healed...

Exposure of the Wound Is Necessary for complete Healing...

Even if it hurts at first, its benefits will be enjoyed in the end...

DON'T HIDE YOUR WOUNDS ANY LONGER!!

... RECEIVE THE HEALING OF YOUR SOUL

www.ingramcontent.com/pod-product-compliance
Lightning Source LLC
LaVergne TN
LVHW010702110826
845149LV00014B/3189

* 9 7 9 8 9 9 3 7 5 6 8 9 9 *